U0088072

MP3

Good morning.
很{生活}的英語

張瑜凌 編著

國家圖書館出版品預行編目資料

Good morning很生活的英語 / 張瑜凌編著
-- 二版 -- 新北市：雅典文化，民106.11
面；　公分. -- (全民學英文；45)
ISBN 978-986-5753-94-8(平裝附光碟片)
1. 英語　　　　2. 會話
805.188　　　　　　　　　106018497

全民學英文系列　45

Good morning很生活的英語

編著／張瑜凌
責任編輯／張瑜凌
美術編輯／王國卿
封面設計／姚恩涵

法律顧問：方圓法律事務所／涂成樞律師

總經銷：永續圖書有限公司
永續圖書線上購物網
www.foreverbooks.com.tw

CVS代理／美璟文化有限公司
TEL：（02）2723-9968
FAX：（02）2723-9668

出版日／2017年11月

雅典文化

出版社
22103　新北市汐止區大同路三段194號9樓之1
TEL　（02）8647-3663
FAX　（02）8647-3660

序言 ....

想要學好英文，
就得從「英文生活化」
開始！

　　學英文的訣竅在哪裡？許多英文學習者都以
為一定要出國才能夠說得一口流利的英文，其實
不然，只要你能創造一個全英文的環境，自然就
有非常多的機會可以開口說英文。

　　想要學好英文，你必須透過「英文生活化」
的學習法，強調利用生活中常見的口語英文，一
天一句，才能打好口語英文的基礎，建立每天都
能開口說英文的環境。

　　如何創造屬於你學習過程中該有的英文環境
呢？本書「Good morning很生活的英語」編列各
種情境用語，讓您可以有多種的學習例句，藉此
豐富英文會話的相關用語。建議您可以以「每天

一個單元」爲學習目標，並隨著本書所附的MP3
學習光碟導讀，讓自己可以跟得上外師導讀的速
度，以加強你的會話熟悉度，英文開口說真輕鬆。

PART

5　問 路　075

PART

6　打電話　095

PART

7　談論天氣　119

PART

8　日期與時間　131

PART
9 關心健康   145

PART
10 談喜好厭惡   161

PART
11 道 歉   179

PART
12 感 謝   195

Unit 1

問 候

問候的問句

★ How do you do?
你好嗎？（初次見面的用語）

★ How are you?
你好嗎？

★ How are you today?
你今天好嗎？

★ How are you this morning?
今早好嗎？

★ How are you, Mr. Jones?
瓊斯先生，你好嗎？

★ How are you doing?
你好嗎？

★ How are things?
一切都好吧？

★ How is everything?
最近還好嗎？

★ How have you been?
你近來好嗎？

★ How has it been going?
近來好嗎？

★ How are you getting on?
你過得怎麼樣？

★ How was your day?
你今天過得如何？

★ How was your week?
你這個星期過得如何？

★ How is your wife?
你的太太好嗎？

★ How is your family?
你的家人好嗎？

★ How is everyone?
大家都過得好嗎？

★ How is your work?
工作進展得如何了？

★ How is school?
今天在學校過得如何？

★ Is everything all right?
事情都順利吧？

回應問候

★ Great.
很好。

★ Not bad.
不錯。

★ OK.
很好。

★ Pretty good.
很好。

★ I'm great.
我很好。

★ I'm all right.
我很好。

★ I'm doing well.
我很好。

★ Fine, thank you.
很好，謝謝。

★ Just fine. Thanks.
還好，謝謝。

★ Very well. How about you?
很好。你呢？

★ All right. And you?
還不錯。你呢？

★ It's going pretty well.
很順利。

★ Still the same.
還是一樣。

★ Same as always.
老樣子。

★ Same as usual.
和平常一樣。

★ Everyone is fine, thank you.
每一個人都很好。謝謝你!

★ Not so good.
沒有那麼好。

★ So-so.
馬馬虎虎。

★ It's terrible.
很糟糕。

★ Not too well. I have a cold.
不太好。我感冒了。

★ It's a hard time for us.
對我們來說是一段難熬的日子。

實·用·會·話·1 ●────────●

A：Hi! How are you?

B：Fine, thanks. And you?

A：Just fine. Nice weather, isn't it?

B：Yes, we've got a warm day.

A：Are you going somewhere?

B：I'm going to downtown. How about you?

B：I'm going to work.

A：OK. I'll see you later.

B：Good-bye.

━ ━ ━ ━ ━ ━ ━ ━ ━ ━ ━ ━ ━ ━

A：嗨！你好嗎？

B：不錯，謝了。你呢？

A：還好。天氣很好，不是嗎？

B：是啊，今天暖和。

A：你要去什麼地方嗎？

B：我要去市中心。你呢？

B：我要去上班。

A：再見囉！

B：再見！

①
問
候

深入分析

1. Nice weather, isn't it? 天氣很好，不是嗎？

歐美人士見面喜歡談論天氣，因為這不涉及個人的隱私，假如外國友人向你說 "It's nice today, isn't it?" 你也不必當真，只要回答 "Yes, it is." 即可，其實這也不算什麼回答，只能算是符合對方的問候，因為天氣好壞任誰都看得出來，他只不過想表示友好而已。

A：Beautiful day, isn't it?
B：Yes. It's not like what the radio said at all.
A：天氣真好，對吧？
B：是啊，和廣播上說的不一樣。

2. We've got a warm day. 天氣真好！

句子中的 have/has got 也等於 have（擁有）的意思，例如：

A：What happened to David?
B：He's got a temperature.
A：大衛怎麼啦？
B：他發燒了。

實·用·會·話·2

A : Hello, David. How are you?

B : Fine, thank you. How about you?

A : Not bad, thanks. You haven't been around much lately, have you?

B : No. I've been away on vacation.

A : Oh? Where were you?

B : Palm Springs. I've got an uncle there. Oh, excuse me, but here comes my bus. Bye.

A : Bye.

━━━━━━━━━━━━━━━━━━━

A：嗨！大衛！你好嗎？

B：很好，謝謝你。你好嗎？

A：還不錯，謝了。你最近都不在對嗎？

B：是不在，我去度假了！

A：是嗎？你去哪裡了？

B：Palm Springs。我有一位叔叔住在那裡。噢，對不起，我的公車來了。再見！

A：再見！

★**Here comes my bus.** 我的公車來了。

在英語中，當 there 或 here 放在句首時，通常使用倒裝句的語法，例如：

⊙There goes the bell.

鈴響了。

但是，如果主詞是人稱代名詞(he/she/it/they/you)，則不能使用倒裝語法，例如：

⊙Here he comes. （非倒裝句）

他來了。

⊙Here comes Chris. （倒裝句）

克里斯來了。

實·用·會·話 3

A：Hello, Jake, I haven't seen you for a long time! Where have you been?

B：Hi, it's you, John. For the past several weeks I was out of town on business matters. I returned only last Monday.

A：You must come over to my house for dinner. We have a lot to talk about. I want to hear all about your trip.

B：It sounds like a good idea. When is a good time to come?

A：How about next Sunday?

B：That's fine with me. See you Sunday.

A：See you.

━ ━ ━ ━ ━ ━ ━ ━ ━ ━ ━ ━ ━ ━

A：你好，傑克，很久沒見了！你跑到那裡去了？

B：嗨，是你啊，約翰。過去幾週我出差去了。上週一才回來。

A：你一定要到我家來吃飯。我們要好好聊聊。我想聽聽你旅途上的事。

B：聽起來是個不錯的主意。什麼時候去好呢？

A：下個星期天怎樣？

B：我可以。星期天見囉！

A：再見！

1. It sounds like a good idea. 聽起來是個不錯的主意。

此句中，it是形式主詞，sounds like 意思是「聽起來……」，例如：

⊙ That sounds nice.

　那聽起來倒是不錯。

⊙ It sounds OK to me.

　對我來說沒有問題。

⊙ It sounds terrible.

　那聽起來很糟糕。

2. How about...? 你認為……如何？

通常用 How about...? 的句型是向他人提出建議，屬於一種徵詢意見的語句，例如：

⊙ How about next Sunday?

　(你覺得)下星期天如何？

⊙ How about going for an outing?

　(你覺得)出去郊遊怎麼樣？

⊙ How about a cup of coffee?

　(你覺得)來杯咖啡如何？

實·用·會·話·4

A：Hello, Peter.

B：Hi, Joy. How are you doing?

A：Great. How about you? Is everyone OK?

B：Everyone is fine except Charlie.

A：Charlie? What happened to him?

B：He broke his leg in a car accident.

A：I'm sorry to hear that. Is it serious?

B：I'm not sure. I'll call him on tonight.

A：Please send my regards to him.

B：I will.

━ ━ ━ ━ ━ ━ ━ ━ ━ ━ ━ ━ ━ ━

A：哈囉，彼得。

B：嗨，喬依。你好嗎？

A：不錯，你呢？大家都好嗎？

B：除了查理之外，大家都不錯。

A：查理？他怎麼啦？

B：他在一場車禍中摔斷腿了。

A：真是遺憾。嚴重嗎？

B：我也不確定。我今晚要去拜訪他。

A：幫我向他問好。

B：我會的！

深入分析

★**Everyone is fine except Charlie.**
除了查理之外,大家都不錯。
except 表示「除了……之外」,可當介系詞
及連接詞使用,例如:
⊙We all go to school except that young girl.
除了那位年輕的女孩之外,我們全都去
上學。
⊙David did nothing except complain while
he was here.
大衛在這裡時,除了抱怨之外,還是抱
怨。

認識新朋友

引薦、介紹

★ I don't think you've met each other before.
我想你們倆以前沒見過面吧！

★ Have you ever met Tom?
你見過湯姆嗎？

★ Have you ever met my husband?
你見過我的先生嗎？

★ Do you know that girl in black?
你認識那位穿黑衣的女孩嗎？

★ Do you know Ruby?
你認識露比嗎？

★ Let me introduce myself.
讓我自我介紹。

★ Allow me to introduce Miss Smith.
我來介紹史密斯小姐。

★ Allow me to introduce you to Mr. Baker.
讓我介紹你給貝克先生認識。

★ David, let me introduce Mr. Jones to you.
大衛，我來介紹一下瓊斯先生給你認識。

★ I'd like to introduce my friend Tom.
我想介紹一下我的朋友湯姆。

★ I'd like you to meet my friend Tom.
我想讓你來見一下我的朋友湯姆。

★ I'd like you to meet a friend of mine.
我希望你見見我的一位朋友。

★ I'd like you to meet my family.
我希望你見見我的家人。

★ I'd like you to meet Mr. Jones, my boss.
我想要你認識瓊斯先生，他是我的老闆。

★ Mary, meet my friend Tom.
瑪麗，來見我的朋友湯姆。

★ Chris, this is Mr. Jones.
克里斯，這是瓊斯先生。

★ Kate, this is Chris. Chris, this is Kate, my sister.
凱特，這是克里斯。克里斯，這是我妹妹凱特。

★ Meet Tom.
來見一下湯姆。

★ Come to meet Tom.
來見見湯姆。

★ I'm Tom Jones, David's boss.
我叫湯姆‧瓊斯，是大衛的老闆。

★ She is my wife Sally.
她是我的太太莎莉。

★ They are my parents. **MP3** 008
他們是我的父母。

★ I'm Sally's sister.
我是莎莉的姐姐。

★ This is Mr. White.
這是懷特先生。

★ They are Mr. and Mrs. White.
他們是懷特夫婦。

★ Tom is an old friend of mine.
湯姆是我的一位老朋友。

介紹後的打招呼

★ Hello.
哈囉!

★ Hi, Tom.
嗨,湯姆。

★ Hello yourself.
你好啊!

★ How do you do?
你好!

★ Glad to meet you.
很高興認識你。

★ Nice to meet you.
很高興認識你。

★ Good to meet you.
很高興認識你。

★ Pleased to meet you.
很高興認識你。

★ Very nice to meet you.
非常高興認識你。

★ I'm pleased to meet you.
我很高興認識你。

★ It's my pleasure to meet you.
  認識你是我的榮幸。

★ Nice to meet you, too.
  我也很高興認識你。

★ I've heard so much about you.
  久仰你的大名。

★ I've heard a lot about you.
  久仰大名。

★ Please call me Tom.
  請叫我湯姆。

★ Just call me Tom.
  叫我湯姆就好了。

實·用·會·話·1

Kate: Oh, I don't think you've met each other be
      fore. Mary, meet my friend Jack. Jack,
      this is Mary.

Mary: Glad to meet you.

Jack: Nice to meet you, too.

Mary: I've heard so much about you.

Jack: Same with me. By the way, how are things
      going with you?

Mary: Everything is OK. How about you?

Jack: I'm very busy now.

Kate: Jack is preparing for an examination.

Mary: Good luck.

Jack: Thank you very much.

- - - - - - - - - - - - - -

凱特：哦，我想你們倆以前沒見過吧。瑪麗，來
　　　見我的朋友，傑克。傑克，這是瑪麗。

瑪麗：很高興認識你。

傑克：我也很高興認識妳。

瑪麗：我已經久仰你的大名了。

傑克：我也是。順便問一下，妳現在好嗎？

瑪麗：一切都好。你呢？

傑克：我現在很忙。

凱特：傑克正在準備考試。

瑪麗：祝你好運。

湯姆：非常感謝。

深入分析

1. Glad to meet you. 很高興能認識你！

meet 除了是「見面」的意思之外，用在介紹的場合時，中文則翻譯為「認識」，而非使用 know，例如：

⊙你如何認識你的太太？

How did you meet your wife? (正)

How did you know your wife? (誤)

2. How are things going with you? 你過得好嗎？

是向人表達關切的話，實際上就相當於 How are you?的問句。

3. How about you? 你呢？

這裏的 How about...?是用來表達關心別人的情況，而且往往用在對方提出問候，而你回答自己的狀況後，才反問對方相同問題的意思，例如：

A：How are you doing?

B：Great. How about you?

A：你好嗎？

B：我很好！你好嗎？

實·用·會·話·2

John: Hi, Lucy. I don't think you've met Jack. Jack is my new roommate. Jack, this is Lucy. Lucy lives next door.

Jack: Nice to meet you, Lucy.

Lucy: Nice to meet you, too, Jack.

- - - - - - - - - - - - - -

約翰：你好，露茜。我想你沒見過傑克吧！傑克是我的新室友。傑克，這是露茜。露茜就住在隔壁。

傑克：很高興認識妳，露茜。

露茜：也很高興認識你，傑克。

深入分析

I don't think you've met Jack. 我想你沒見過傑克吧！

"I don't think..." 是一句非常普遍的句型，表示「我不認為…」，但在翻譯成中文時，通常可以解釋為「我覺得…不…」，例如：

A：I don't think you would understand.

B：Why not?

A：我覺得你不會瞭解。

B：為什麼不會？

實·用·會·話·3

A：Kate, may I present Dr. John Wells, our guest speaker for today. Dr. Wells, this is Kate.

Kate: How do you do?

John: I'm pleased to meet you.

A：Kate will introduce you to the audience today.

John: I'm honored.

Kate：It's my pleasure.

A：凱特，我可以介紹今天的演講來賓嗎？

約翰·威爾斯博士。威爾斯博士，這是凱特。

凱特：你好。

約翰：很高興能認識妳。

A：凱特將把你介紹給今天的聽眾。

約翰：我感到很榮幸。

凱特：我很高興這麼做。

深入分析

How do you do? 你好嗎？

通常用在初次認識，而且多用於正式場合見面之時，一般生活中則不拘於小節，往往一句 "Hi" 就可達到初次見面的打招呼目的了。

A：How do you do?

B：Good. How about you?

A：你好嗎？

B：很好！你呢？

實·用·會·話·4

A：Hello.

B：Hello yourself.

A：My name is David.

B：I'm Susan.

A：Where are you from?

B：I'm from Taiwan.

A：What's your impression of the United States?

B：Well, I can't get over how different weat h e r is here.

A：Oh, you'll get used to it soon.

A：哈囉！

B：哈囉！

A：我的名字叫大衛。

B：我是蘇珊。

A：你從哪兒來？

B：我來自台灣。

A：你對美國有什麼看法？

B：是這樣的，我對於天氣變化實在是不習慣。

A：喔！你很快就會習慣的。

MP3 012

實·用·會·話·5 •

A：Kate, this is Mr. Brown. Kate is our new copywrite.

B：Good to meet you, Mr. Brown.

C：It's good to meet you, too. How do you find things over here?

B：It's quite different from what I expected.

C：Don't worry, you'll get used to it soon.

A：凱特，這是布朗先生。凱特是我們的新進的文案人員。

B：非常高興見到你，布朗先生。

C：我也是。妳覺得這裏怎麼樣？

B：與我所想像的十分不同。

C：別擔心，妳很快就會習慣的。

1. A be different from B　A 和 B 同

是固定搭配的用法，意思是「A 與 B 不同」，例如：

⊙ Your method is different from mine.

　你的方法與我的不同。

⊙ This book is different from that one in color.

　這本書與那本書的顏色不同。

2. You'll get used to it.　你會習慣的。

"get used to..." 意思是「變得習慣於...」，這裏的 "to" 是介詞，後面要接名詞、代詞或動名詞，例如：

⊙ Susan got used to living alone after her husband died.

　自從丈夫死後，蘇珊習慣了獨自生活。

⊙ He hasn't got used to life in Taipei.

　他還不習慣台北的生活。

此外，可以在句尾加上時間副詞 soon、in a few days、before long 等，以說明要習慣此狀況的時間長短，例如：

A：The weather is really different here.

B：You'll get used to it in a few days.

A：這裡的天氣真的不太一樣。

B：過一陣子你就會習慣的。

Unit 3

閒聊的客套用語

客套用語

★ I'm pleased to see you again.
很高興再看見你。

★ Nice to see you again.
很高興再看見你。

★ Nice to see you.
見到你真好。

★ Good to see you again.
好高興又再見到你。

★ I'm so happy to see you.
我很高興見到你。

★ Nice weather, isn't it?
天氣很好，不是嗎？

★ Hey, what's going on here?
嘿，這裡發生什麼事了？

★ I'm sorry to hear that.
我很遺憾聽見這件事。

★ I'm glad for you.
我很為你高興。

★ I'm proud of you.
我為你感到驕傲。

寒暄

★ What a surprise!
多讓人驚奇呀！

★ What a shame!
多可惜呀！

★ What a fine day!
多好的天氣呀！

★ What a coincidence!
多巧啊！

★ It has been a long time.
真是好久了！（指時間過得真快）

★ Long time no see.
好久不見！

★ I haven't seen you for weeks.
好幾個星期沒見到你了！

★ I haven't seen you for months.
好幾個月沒見到你了！

★ I haven't seen you for ages.
真是好久不見了！

★ I haven't seen you for a long time.
我有好久沒見你了！

❸ 閒聊的客套用語

★ You haven't changed at all.
你一點都沒變。

★ You look beautiful.   🎵 014
你看起來很漂亮。

★ You look great.
你看起來氣色不錯。

★ You look fantastic.
你看起來漂亮極了！

★ You look very happy.
你看起來很高興。

★ You look a bit tired.
你看起來有點累了。

★ You look terrible.
你看起來糟透了。

★ You look pale.
你看起來臉色蒼白。

★ Where are you off to?
你要去哪裡？

★ Where are you going?
你要去那裡？

★ What's the hurry?
你在趕什麼？

★ What are you doing here?
你在這裡做什麼？

★ Are you coming alone?
你自己來嗎？

★ I've been away on a business trip.
我去出差了。

★ I've been away on vacation.
我去度假了。

★ I've been away to New York.
我去了紐約。

★ I've been away doing shopping.
我出去買東西了。

★ I've been in California for the past 2 months.
過去二個月我都在加州。

★ I went to New York for a few weeks.
我這幾個星期去了一趟紐約。

③ 閒聊的客套用語

實·用·會·話·1

A：Hi, Maggie.

B：David! Have a seat.

A：Thanks.

B：Nice to see you again.

A：Me too. Do you work around here?

B：Yes, I work at Hyatt Hotel.

-- -- -- -- -- -- -- -- -- -- -- -- --

A：嗨！瑪姬。

B：大衛！請坐。

A：謝謝！

B：很高興又見到你。

A：我也是。妳在這裡工作嗎？

B：是啊！我在君悅飯店工作。

深入分析

Have a seat. 請坐。

「請人坐下」的說法有許多種，"Have a seat" 是比較隨性的用法，其他的說法還有以下幾種：

⊙ Take a seat.

請坐。

⊙ Sit down, please.

請坐。

⊙ Sit.

坐！

實·用·會·話 2

A：David?

B：Maggie! What are you doing here?

A：I visited one of my friends around here.

B：How are you doing?

A：Still the same. And you? You look great.

B：I just got married last week.

A：Realy? Congratulations.

B：Thanks.

A：大衛？

B：瑪姬！妳在這裡作什麼？

A：我來附近拜訪一位朋友。

B：妳好嗎？

A：老樣子。你呢？你看起來氣色不錯耶！

B：我上個禮拜剛結婚了。

A：真的嗎？恭喜你！

B：謝謝！

016

0
5
1

1. get married　結婚

「婚姻」是人生轉變的一個重要過程，「婚姻」是 marriage，而「結婚」的動詞則是 marry，相關用法如下：

⊙He married Maggie last month.

他上個月和瑪姬結婚了。

⊙They got married in 2003.

他們是 2003 年結婚的。

2. Congratulations.　恭喜你！

Congratulations 是一種慣用法，表示很多的恭喜，所以是用複數形態表示。此外，常見的祝福用語，則可以用 "Good luck" 表示，例如：

A：Wish me luck.

B：Good luck.

A：祝我好運！

B：祝你好運！

3 閒聊的客套用語

實·用·會·話·3

A：Hi, Kate.

B：Oh, hi, David.

A：What's wrong? You look upset.

B：I just got a lay off.

A：I'm so sorry to hear that.

B：It's OK. I'm looking for a job now.

A：嗨，凱特。

B：噢，嗨，大衛。

A：怎麼啦？妳看起來心情不好

B：我被遣散了。

A：我很遺憾聽到這件事。

B：沒關係。我現在正在找工作。

MP3 017

實·用·會·話·4

A：Say, aren't you Tony Hudson?

B：Yes. That's right. Do I know you?

A：Didn't you attend the party last night?

B：Yes, but I....

A：Well, we were introduced before the party. I'm Bob Andrews.

B：Oh, yes! How could I forget! You were with a blond lady then.

- - - - - - - - - - - - - - - -

A：嘿，你是湯尼·哈德遜嗎？

B：是的，我認識你嗎？

A：你不是參加了昨晚的聚會了嗎？

B：參加了，但我……

A：呃，我們是聚會之前經介紹認識的。我叫鮑勃·安德魯斯。

B：天哪，我怎麼會忘了呢？你當時是和一位金髮女郎在一起的。

深入分析

1. Say, ... 嘿，...

say 是「說話」的意思，在口語化中則是「喂、等等、那個」的意思，有感嘆之意的用語，例如：

A：Say, why don't we go to see a movie?

B：Sounds great. Come on, let's go.

A：喂，要不要去看電影？

B：聽起來不錯喔！走吧！

2. Do I know you? 我認識你嗎？

這句 "Do I know you?" 通常適用在對方突然和你說話，而你卻不確定是否認識對方時使用，表示希望對方提示你彼此是如何認識的。但若是你提出彼此似乎是認識的寒暄用語，則可以說 "Do I know you from some-where?"，表示「我們好像在哪裡見過面吧？」例如：

A：Do I know you from somewhere?

B：I am John's wife.

A：我們好像在哪裡見過面吧？

B：我是約翰的太太。

MP3 018

實·用·會·話·5 ●---------------------●

A： Why don't we just...

B： Look, who's here. Susan!

C： Hey, Peter. Fancy meeting you here.
I thought you were abroad.

A： We just got back. It's nice to see you both
here. What a coincidence!

B： We're here on holiday. Tell me how was
your trip to America.

— — — — — — — — — — — — — — — —

A：我們何不…

B：你瞧那是誰？蘇珊！

C：嘿，彼得！沒想到會在這兒見到你。我以為
你們出國了。

A：我們剛剛回來。在這兒見到你們二位真高
興。多巧啊！

B：我們是來度假的。告訴我們你美國之行的事
吧！

深入分析

1. **I thought...** 我以為……

   當某事與預期中不相符時使用，後面的子句
   必須用過去式表示，例如：

   ⊙I thought she was mad at me.

   我以為她在生我的氣。

2. **Fancy meeting you here.** 很訝異會在這裡
   遇見你。

   這裏的fancy用於感歎語氣，表示驚訝，例
   如：

   ⊙Fancy her saying such unkind things about
   you!

   她竟然說出這些對你無情的話！

   ⊙Just fancy! How strange!

   多奇怪呀！真想不到！

3. **What a coincidence!** 好巧喔！

   What a coincidence!是感歎句，意思是「多
   麼巧合呀」，多用於巧遇時或發生某件令人
   不得不相信的巧合之事。常用句型為"what
   a …"，表示「多麼地…」，例如：

   ⊙What a surprise!

   真是令人驚訝！

   ⊙What a fine day.

   天氣真好！

實·用·會·話·6

A：Hello, Jack! Fancy meeting you here! How are you these days?

B：Fine, just fine. And you?

A：Things couldn't be better. And how's Jim doing?

B：He's the same. You know him, always busy, in the office or at home.

A：Oh, Jim. Look, I'm late for work. I'll call you sometime later, but now I should get going.

B：All right. See you!

3
閒聊的客套用語

A：你好，傑克！真沒想到在這兒見到你。近來好嗎？

B：好，很好。你呢？

A：非常好。吉姆怎樣？

B：他還是老樣子。你知道的，他總是很忙的，不是在辦公室忙，就是在家裏忙。

A：哎，吉姆這傢伙。哦，我上班要遲到了。我再打電話給你，但現在我得走了。

B：好的，再見！

深入分析

1. Things couldn't be better. 事情再好不過了！

"couldn't be better" 這種否定形式接形容詞的比較級句型，通常帶有「極端」的意味，這句話的意思是「不能再好了」，例如：

⊙ The traffic jam couldn't be worse.

交通阻塞真是糟透了！

2. Look! 聽我說。

這是一句相當口語化的說法，並不是要對方「看」，而是引起對方注意的一種語助詞，有點類似中文「聽著，…」，例如：

A：It's my fault.

B：Look! Don't blame yourself.

A：都是我的錯！

B：聽我說，你別責怪你自己了。

A：I think I've seen you before.

B：No, I don't think so.

A：Aren't you Robert Jones? I believe we met at a sales conference last summer.

B：Yes. Now I remember. You're an engineer. What a coincidence!

A：You know what they say. It's a small world.

B：Perfectly right. Ha, ha, ha....

— — — — — — — — — — — — — — — —

A：我想我以前見過你。

B：不，沒有吧。

A：你不是叫羅勃特‧瓊斯嗎？我相信我們是去年夏天在一次銷售會議上認識的。

B：對，我想起來了。你是一位工程師。真巧啊！

A：你知道人們是怎麼說的：「這世界真小」。

B：完全正確。哈哈哈……！

3

閒聊的客套用話

實·用·會·話·8

A：Hello, Maggie.

B：Oh, Mr. White. How have you been?

A：Pretty good, thank you.

B：You look a bit tired.

A：It's nothing. I was up late last night.

────────────────

A：瑪姬，妳好！

B：噢，懷特先生。你好嗎？

A：很好，謝謝。

B：你看起來有點累。

A：沒事，我昨晚太晚睡了。

深入分析

> ★**be up late 熬夜**
>
> 相同的「熬夜」用法意思還包括 "stay
> up"，例如：
>
> A：Don't stay up so late. You have to go to
> work tomorrow.
>
> B：I won't.
>
> A：不要熬夜太晚。你明天還要工作。
>
> B：我不會的！

A：What a surprise! Meeting you here.

B：I haven't seen you for ages. Where have you been?

A：I've been away on a business trip.

B：Where did you go?

A：Japan.

B：Listen, maybe we can have some coffee together...

A：I'd love to, but I've to catch the 9:00 plane.

B：OK. Maybe some other time.

A：Yeah. See you.

❸ 閒聊的客套用語

━━━━━━━━━━━━━━

A：真沒想到，我們會在這裡見面！

B：好久沒見面了，你去哪兒去了？

A：我去出差了。

B：去哪裡出差？

A：日本。

B：聽著，也許我們可以一起喝杯咖啡。

A：我是很想，可是我要趕搭九點鐘的班機。

B：好吧，那就以後再找時間吧！

A：好啊！再見囉！

深入分析

1. I haven't seen you for ages. 好久沒看見你了！

for ages 也等於 for a long time，表示「很久」，例如：

A：We've been waiting for ages.

B：My mistake, sir.

A：我們已經等很久了。

B：抱歉，先生，都是我的錯！

2. Maybe some other time. 以後再找時間吧！

若是對方提出邀約，而你無法答應，對方就可以說 "Maybe some other time." ，是一種替自己找台階下的用語，若是你的確不想接受邀約，此時只要回應說 sure 或 yeah，但是你若是真的願意再找時間赴約，也可以直接回應 "How about+時間" ，例如：

A：Wanna come with us?

B：I'd love to, but I can't.

A：Maybe some other time.

B：How about tomorrow?

A：Good. I'll pick you up at five.

A：要不要和我們一起去？

B：我是很想去，可是我去不了。

A：那就以後再找時間吧！

B：明天可以嗎？

A：好啊！我五點鐘來接你。

道別

說再見

★ Bye-bye.
再見！

★ Goodbye.
再見！

★ See you.
再見！

★ See you later.
待會見。

★ See you around.
待會見！

★ See you Sunday.
星期日見！

★ See you tomorrow.
明天見！

★ See you next time.
下次見！

★ I'll see you sometime.
下次見！

★ I think I should be going.
我想我要走了。

★ I have to go.
　我必須走了。

★ I have got to go.
　我必須走了。

★ I really have to go.
　我真的要走了。

★ I hate to say goodbye.
　我討厭說再見。

★ I have come to say goodbye.
　我順道來說一聲再見。

★ I'd like to say goodbye to everyone.
　再見了，各位。

★ Let's go home.
　我們回家吧！

★ It's getting late.
　時候不早了。

約定再見面

★ See you at 10 o'clock.
十點鐘見。

★ See you at the lounge.
大廳見。

★ See you again next week.
下星期再見！

★ Hope to see you soon.
希望能很快地再見到你。

★ I hope we meet again soon.
希望我們不久後能夠盡快再見面。

★ I hope to see you soon again.
希望很快再見到你。

★ I can't wait to see you again.
我等不及再看到你。

★ Let's get together again soon.
我們盡快再找個時間聚一聚吧！

★ Let's get together sometime.
有空聚一聚吧！

★ If you're ever in Taipei, you must look me up.
如果你來台北，一定要來拜訪我。

聯絡方式

★ Do you have a cellular phone?
  你有手機嗎？

★ How do I contact you?
  我要如何聯絡你？

★ This is my business card.
  這是我的名片。

★ Here is my e-mail address.
  這是我的電子郵件信箱。

★ Let me write down your phone number.
  我來寫下你的電話號碼。

保持聯絡

★ Give me a call when you're in town.
如果你進城，打個電話給我。

★ Call me when you arrive in Taiwan.
到台灣時打個電話給我。

★ Give me a call sometime.
偶爾給我個電話吧。

★ Call me sometime.
偶爾打個電話給我吧！

★ Please call me anytime you like.
隨時都可以打電話給我。

★ Don't forget to keep in touch.
別忘了要保持聯絡。

★ Let's keep in touch.
保持聯絡。

★ Don't forget to write.
別忘了寫信（給我）。

★ Write me sometime.
有空寫信給我。

★ Meet you on line.
線上再見囉！

祝福用語

★ Good luck.
  祝你好運。

★ Good luck to you.
  祝你好運。

★ Take care.
  保重。

★ Take care of yourself, my friend.
  我的朋友，請保重。

★ Goodbye and have a good trip.
  再見，祝你一路順風。

★ Have a good flight back.
  祝你回程旅途平安。

★ Have a good trip.
  祝你旅途平安。

★ Please say hello to Mr. White for me.
  請幫我向懷特先生打招呼。

★ Please give my best regards to your mother.
  請幫我向你母親問好。

臨別前的客套話用語

★ It was really fun hanging out with you.
跟你相處真是有意思。

★ Nice talking to you.
很高興和你聊天。

★ Have a nice day.
祝你有美好的一天。

★ Don't work too hard.
不要工作太累。

★ Take it easy.
放輕鬆點。

★ I'll miss you.
我會想念你的。

A：So you will call Mr. Jones, won't you?

B：Yes, I have to.

A：Don't worry about it. It's no big deal.

B：Thanks. I have to go now. Bye.

A：See you next time.

- - - - - - - - - - - - - - - -

A：所以你會打電話給瓊斯先生，對吧？

B：是的，我必須要。

A：別擔心，沒什麼大不了的。

B：謝啦！我要走了，再見！

A：再見！

深入分析

See you next time.　再見！

　　美國人說「再見」有許多種方式，see you next time 是單純「再見」的意思，並不一定表示兩人已約好下次見面的時間了，所以下次聽到美國人說 see you next time 時，可別會錯意以為雙方還有約而追問對方：When？（什麼時候）

實·用·會·話·2

A：Just leave me alone.

B：Let me help you. Please?

A：No, I can manage it myself.

B：OK. Can I go home now?

A：Sure. See you tomorrow.

- - - - - - - - - - - - - - -

A：不用管我！

B：讓我幫你吧！拜託啦！

A：沒有，我可以自己處理。

B：好吧！現在我可以走了嗎？

A：好啊！明天見囉！

深入分析

Please? 拜託啦！

Please 除了是一般人廣為熟知的「請」的禮
貌用語之外，也有「拜託」、「請求」的意
思，例如：

A：Give me the key.

B：That's it?

A：That's it. Please?

A：給我鑰匙。

B：就這樣？

A：就這樣。拜託啦！

實·用·會·話 3

A：Where are you going?

B：Taipei Railway Station.

A：It's on my way home.

B：Really? Can you give me a lift?

A：Sure. Get in.

(Later)

A：Here we are.

B：Thanks. See you later.

A：Bye and take care.

- - - - - - - - - - - - - -

A：你要去哪裡？

B：台北車站。

A：在我回家的路上。

B：真的嗎？你能讓我搭便車去嗎？

A：當然好，上車吧！

（稍後）

A：我們到了。

B：謝啦！再見！

A：拜拜，小心喔！

4 道別

深入分析

give sb. a lift 讓某人搭便車

　　lift 表示抬起、舉起之意，而「讓人搭便車」除了 give sb. a lift 之外，相同意思還有 give sb. a ride 的用法。

A：Could anybody give me a lift there and back?

B：I can do that.

A：有沒有人能送我過去和回來？

B：我可以。

A：Wanna a ride?

B：Really? Thank you so much.

A：要搭便車嗎？

B：真的嗎？太感謝你了。

Unit 5

問 路

問路

★ I'm lost.
　我迷路了。

★ Where am I on the map?
　我在地圖上的哪裡?

★ What street am I on?
　我在哪一條街上?

★ Can I get some directions?
　能問一下路嗎?

★ Excuse me, where is the Museum?
　請問一下,博物館在哪裡?

★ Do you know where the Museum is?
　你知道博物館在哪裡嗎?

★ Where is the nearest gas station?
　最近的加油站在哪裡?

★ Excuse me, could you tell me the way to the station?
　請問一下,你能告訴我去車站的路嗎?

★ Excuse me, could you show me the way to the station?
　請問一下,你能指點我去車站的路嗎?

★ Excuse me, but where is the station?
請問一下，車站在哪兒？

★ Excuse me, could you tell me how I can get to the station?
請問一下，你能告訴我要如何到車站嗎？

★ How can I get to the station?
我要如何到車站呢？

★ Is this the road to the station?
這是去車站的路嗎？

★ Excuse me, does this street lead to the station?
請問，這條街是通往車站嗎？

★ What's the name of this road?
這條路是什麼路名？

★ How far is it from here?
從這裡去有多遠？

★ How long does it take on foot?
走路要多久的時間？

★ Can I walk there?
我可以走路過去嗎？

★ Shall I take a taxi?
我應該要搭計程車嗎？

★ Can you direct me to the police office?
你能告訴我去警察局怎麼走嗎？

★ Where is the entrance to TICC?
台北國際會議中心的入口在哪裡？

★ How can I get to this address?　　　　MP3 028
我要怎麼到這個地址？

★ Are there any landmarks on the way?
路上有沒有任何的路標？

★ Which side of the street is it on?
在街道的哪一邊？

★ Where can I take a taxi?
我可以在哪裡招到計程車？

★ Where can I buy the ticket?
我要去哪裡買車票？

★ Which train goes to New York?
哪一班車有到紐約？

★ Is the right line for New York?
去紐約是這條路線嗎？

★ Is this the right platform for New York?
這是出發到紐約的月台嗎？

★ Where should I transfer to get to New York?

我要去哪裡轉車到紐約？

★ Where should I change trains for New York?

我要去哪裡換車到紐約？

★ Where should I get off to go to New York?

到紐約要在哪裡下車？

★ Does this bus go to New York?

這班公車有到紐約嗎？

★ Is this bus stop for New York?

這個站牌有到紐約嗎？

★ Does this bus stop at City Hall?

這班公車有停靠在市政府嗎？

★ How often does this bus run?

公車多久來一班？

★ How many stops are there to Taipei?

到台北有多少個站？

★ What's the next station?

下一站是哪裡？

★ Which stop is nearest to City Hall?

哪一站最靠近市政府？

5
問
路

★ I missed my stop.
我錯過站下車了。

MP3 029

指引方向

★ It's on the right.
在右邊。

★ It's on your right.
在你的右手邊。

★ Turn right at the second crossing.
在第二個十字路口向右轉。

★ Turn left when you see the T-junction.
看到T形路口，就向左轉。

★ Take the second right.
在第二個路口右轉。

★ Take a number 11 bus and get off at the Zoo.
搭乘11路公車，到動物園下車。

★ It's across from City Hall.
就在市政府對面。

★ It's next to the school.
就在學校旁邊。

★ The post office is just across from the school.

郵局就在學校的對面。

★ It's on the opposite of the post office.

就在郵局的對面。

★ The school is opposite to the post office.

學校就在郵局的對面。

★ It's between the school and the post office.

就在學校和郵局之間。

★ It's on the right side of the school.

就在學校的右邊。

★ It's in front of the school.

就在學校的前面。

★ Go straight ahead and then take the first turn on the left.

一直向前走，然後在第一個路口向左轉。

★ Go straight for three blocks.

向前走三個街區就到了。

★ Go straight along this street.

沿著這條街向前走。

★ Go straight along this street for two blocks.

沿著這條街向前走兩個街區。

★ Go straight ahead about four blocks and turn left.
直走過四個街區再左轉。

★ Go straight ahead until you see the traffic light.
直走到紅綠燈為止。

★ Turn right at the second traffic light.
在第二個紅綠燈處右轉。

★ Turn left and you will see it on your right side.   MP3 030
左轉後，你就會看到在你的右手邊。

★ You will see it at the corner on your right.
你會看到在你右手邊的轉角處。

★ You are here.
你在這裡。

★ You are going the wrong way.
你走錯方向了。

★ You can get there on foot.
你可以走路過去。

★ You'd better take a bus.
你最好搭公車。

★ I'm going there myself. Follow me, please.
我正要去那兒。請跟我來。

★ I'll walk you there. It's on my route.
我會帶你過去。我正好路過那裡。

★ It's about half a mile from here.
離這裡大約半英里。

★ It's not far. Just two blocks away.
不遠。離這裡只有兩個街區。

★ It's about ten minutes' walk.
步行大約需要十分鐘。

★ It takes just five minutes' walk.
走路需要五分鐘。

★ It is a five-minute walk.
走路需要五分鐘。

★ It's about ten minutes' ride from here.
從這裡搭車大約要十分鐘。

★ You won't miss it.
你不會找不到的。

★ It's not far.
不遠。

★ It's pretty close.
很近。

★ It's far away from here.
離這裡很遠。

實·用·會·話·1 ●───────────●

A : Excuse me, sir, but could you please tell me how to get to the police station?

B : Well, it's a long way from here. You should go ahead to the crossroad, then turn right. After 10 minutes' walk, you'll see a hospital. The police station is just opposite it.

A : Oh, it is far, isn't it?

B : Yes, but you can take the No. 11 bus. It will take you right there. The bus stop is just over there.

A : Thank you so much.

B : You're welcome.

— — — — — — — — — — — — — — —

A：對不起，先生，請問到警察局怎麼走？

B：噢，離這兒很遠耶！看，你一直走，走到那個十字路口，然後向右轉，再走十分鐘，你會看到一家醫院，警察局就在那家醫院對面。

A：噢，很遠，對嗎？

B：是的，不過你可以搭乘 11 號公車，它有到那裡。公車站就在那邊。

A：太感謝你了。

B：不客氣。

深入分析

1. Excuse me, ... 打擾一下…

英語中「問路」時通常要用 "Excuse me, ..." 開頭，以示禮貌，有「請問、打擾、麻煩你」的意思，也可以是請對方「借過」時使用，例如：

A：Excuse me, may I ask you a question?

B：Sure.

A：抱歉，我能問你一個問題嗎？

B：可以啊！

2. go ahead 一直走

go ahead 若用在指示方向或行走的場合，表示「一直走」，例如：

A：How can I get to this address?

B：Go ahead till you get to the second crossing.

A：我要怎麼到這個地址？

B：一直走到第二個十字路口。

go ahead 也可以是「好的」或「鼓勵繼續」（行為或說話）的意思，例如：

A：May I ask you a question?

B：Go ahead.

A：我能問你一個問題嗎？

B：說吧！

實·用·會·話·2 ●━━━━━━━━━━━━━━━●

A：Can I help you?

B：Yes. I'm trying to find the B. H. Supermarket. I've been told it is somewhere near here, but I've been walking for a while now and can't seem to find it.

A：Oh, it's right near here. Just walk across the street and go around the corner on Green Road. Walk one block east, take a right at 20th, and then walk about half a block. It's right in the middle of the block.

B：Would you mind drawing me a little map on this piece of paper?

A：No problem, it is easier to follow a map.

B：Is there any landmark there?

A：Oh, yes. You'll see a big apple poster. You can't miss it.

━ ━ ━ ━ ━ ━ ━ ━ ━ ━ ━ ━ ━

A：我能幫你什麼忙嗎？

B：是的。我正在找 B.H.超級市場。有人告訴我它就在這附近。可是我已經找了好一會兒了，好像找不到。

A：哦，就在這附近。你只要橫過馬路，在格林大道拐角處繞過去向東走一個街區。在第二

十街向右轉，然後走大約半個街區。B.H.超
級市場就在那一區的中間。

B：請你在這張紙上幫我畫張路線圖好嗎？

A：沒問題。有路線圖容易找些。

- - - - - - - - - - - - - -

B：那個地方有路標嗎？

A：有的。你會看到一張大蘋果的海報。你不會
找不著的。

深入分析

★Would you mind...?　你介意……嗎？

"Would you…" 句型是一種客氣的用語，
經常用來向他人請求幫忙，是一種比較禮貌
的說法，例如：

A：Would you mind doing me a favor?

B：Yes, I do mind.

A：你介意幫我個忙嗎？

B：不要！

A：Would you mind closing the window?

B：No.

A：你介意把窗戶關上嗎？

B：不介意。

實·用·會·話·3

A：Excuse me. Could you please tell me how to get to the station?

B：Turn left at the first light. You can't miss it.

A：Will it take me long to get there?

B：No. It's not far away.

A：Thank you.

B：Don't mention it.

━━━━━━━━━━━━━━━━━

A：請問一下，到火車站怎麼走？

B：在第一個紅綠燈向左轉。你不會找不著的。

A：要花很久的時間到那裡嗎？

B：不會，不會遠。

A：謝謝你。

B：不客氣。

★**Will it take me long to get there?**
　到那裡會花我很多時間嗎？

若是指「做某件是要花多少時間」的陳述語
句，可以用 "it takes sb.+時間+ to do..."
的句型，it 表示「某件事」，例如：

⊙It'll take me a month to finish this job.
　做完這工作需要花我一個月的時間。

⊙It took me two hours to get there.
　我花了二個小時的時間到達那裡。

若是表示「我花了……(時間)完成某
事」，動詞則不用take，而是用spend表
示，例如：

⊙I spend two hours to finish it.
　我花了二個小時的時間完成那件事。

實·用·會·話·4

A：Does this bus go to the beach?

B：No. You're going the wrong way. You have to take the Number 10. It stops in front of the post office.

A：About how long does it take?

B：Only 10 minutes.

A：Good. Thanks a lot.

B：No problem.

- - - - - - - - - - - - - -

A：這班公車有到海灘嗎？

B：沒有。你走錯路了。你要搭 10 號公車。

A：搭車要多久的時間？

B：只要十分鐘。

A：太好了！多謝啦！

B：不客氣！

take a bus 搭公車

一般說來，搭公車、計程車等是用動詞 take，例如：

⊙Why don't you take a taxi?

你何不搭計程車？

⊙Where should I take the bus?

我要到哪裡搭公車？

A：Excuse me.

B：What can I do for you?

A：Does this bus go to the train station?

B：No. You'll have to get off at the bank and take the A12.

A：How long is the ride?

B：About 20 minutes.

A：I see. Thank you so much.

B：You're quite welcome.

───────────────────

A：請問一下！

B：我能幫你什麼忙？

A：這班公車有到火車站嗎？

B：沒有！你要在銀行下車，然後搭 A12。

A：車程大概要多久？

B：大約廿分鐘。

A：我瞭解了！太感謝你了！

B：不客氣！

深入分析

get off 下車

若是要下車，就可以用片語 "get off"，例如：

⊙ We should get off at the park.

　我們應該在公園下車。

實·用·會·話·6 　　　　　　　　　　 🅼🅿 035

A：Do you need help?

B：Oh, yes. I'm lost. I don't know where I am.

A：Where are you going?

B：I'm going to this place.

A：The Hilton Hotel?

B：That's right. Is it far?

A：Yes, it's very far from here. You'd better take a bus or taxi.

－－－－－－－－－－－－－－－－－－－

A：你需要幫助嗎？

B：喔，對！我迷路了！我不知道我人在哪裡。

A：你要去哪裡？

B：我要去這個地方。

A：（要去）希爾頓飯店？

B：沒錯！很遠嗎？

A：對，離這裡很遠。你最好搭公車或計程車。

I don't know where I am. 我不知道我人在
哪裡！

當人迷路時，是最惶惶不安的，此時你除了
可以說 "I'm lost." 之外，也可以說 "I don't
know where I am."，表示「我不知道自己
身處的這條街道是哪裡」的意思，例如：

A：Do you need help?

B：Yes. I don't know where I am.

A：你需要幫忙嗎？

B：是的！我不知道我人在哪裡！

5
問
路

打電話

去電

★ May I speak to Tom?
我能和湯姆說話嗎？

★ May I speak to Tom, please?
請找湯姆接電話好嗎？

★ Could I talk to Tom or David?
我可以找湯姆或是大衛說話嗎？

★ Is Tom there?
湯姆在嗎？

★ Is that Tom?
你是湯姆嗎？

★ Is Tom in, please?
請問湯姆在家嗎？

★ Is Tom in today?
湯姆今天在嗎？

★ Extension 747, please.
請轉分機747。

★ I want to speak to Tom.
我想和湯姆通話。

★ This is Jake calling for Tom.
我是傑克，打電話來要找湯姆。

★ Is Tom in yet?
湯姆回來了嗎？

★ Is Tom off the line?
湯姆講完電話了嗎？

★ Is Tom in the office now?
湯姆現在在辦公室裡嗎？

★ Is this Tom?
你是湯姆嗎？

★ Do you know when he will be back?
你知道他什麼時候會回來？

★ May I leave a message?
我可以留言嗎？

★ I'll call back later.
我待會再來電。

★ When should I call back?
我什麼時候可以再打來呢？

★ Would you ask him to call Jim at 8647-3663?
你能請他打電話到 8647-3663 給吉姆嗎？

★ Would you tell him Jack returned his call?
請你告訴他，傑克有回他電話。

★ Tell him to give me a call as soon as possible.
告訴他盡快回我電話。

★ Do you know where I can reach him?
你知道我在哪裡可以聯絡上他嗎？　　🎵 037

接電話

★ This is Dr. Ford.
我就是福特教授。

★ This is he.
我就是本人。（說話者為男性）

★ This is she.
我就是本人。（說話者為女性）

★ Speaking.
請說。

★ Mark here.
我是馬克。

★ This is Bob speaking.
我是鮑伯。

★ What is the name of the person you are calling?

你要通話的人是什麼名字？

★ What is the number you are calling?

你打幾號？

★ I can't talk to you now.

我現在不能講（電話）。

★ Let me get back to you in a few minutes.

我幾分鐘後回你電話。

★ Would you mind calling back later?

你可以待會再打電話來嗎？　　　　MP3 038

★ Who is this?

你是哪位？

★ May I ask who is calling?

請問你是哪位？

★ Who is speaking, please?

請問你是哪位？

轉接電話

★ Hold on.
請等一下。

★ Wait a moment, please.
請稍等。

★ Just a moment, please.
請等一下。

★ Would you please wait a moment?
能請你等一下嗎？

★ Hold the line, please.
請稍等不要掛電話。

★ Can you hold?
你可以稍等嗎？

★ Let me see for you.
我幫你看看。

★ Let me see if she is in.
讓我確認一下她在不在。

★ Let me see if he is available.
讓我確認一下他現在有沒有空。

★ I'll find out if he is in the office.
我會確認他是不是在辦公室。

★ He's not in yet.
他現在還不在。

★ He's out to lunch.
他出去用午餐了。

★ He's off today.
他今天休假。

★ He's in a meeting now.
他現在正在開會中。

★ He's in the middle of something.
他正在忙。

★ He's busy with another line.
他正在忙線中。

★ He's still on the phone.
他還在講電話。

★ He won't be free until eleven thirty.
他十一點卅分前都不會有空。

★ The line is busy.
電話占線中。

★ Would you like to leave a message?
你需要留言嗎？

★ Could I take a message?
我能幫你留言嗎？

★ May I tell him who is calling?
需要我告訴他是誰來電嗎？

★ I'll have him return your call.
我會請他回你電話。

★ I'll get him.
我去叫他（來聽電話）。

★ I'll put you through to him immediately.
我立刻幫你轉給他。

★ I'll put your call through.
我替你轉電話。

★ Thank you for waiting.
謝謝你等這麼久。

★ Sorry to have kept you waiting.
抱歉讓你久等了。

實·用·會·話·1

A：Hello, is Jenny in?

B：No, I'm afraid she's out at the moment. Who is speaking, please?

A：Maggie, her friend from Taiwan. May I leave a message?

B：Certainly. Just a moment, please. I need to get a pencil. OK. What is it, please?

A : Would you please tell her to call back this afternoon? I'll be expecting her call then.

B : What's your number?

A : 86473663. Thank you very much.

B : You're welcome.

━ ━ ━ ━ ━ ━ ━ ━ ━ ━ ━ ━ ━ ━

A：喂，珍妮在嗎？

B：不，她現在還沒回來。請問妳是哪一位？

A：我是瑪姬，她的台灣朋友。我可以留言嗎？

B：當然可以。請稍等。我需要支鉛筆。好啦，請問要留什麼話？

A：請你告訴她今天下午給我回個電話好嗎？我會等她的電話。

B：妳的電話號碼是多少？

A：86473663。非常感謝。

B：不必客氣。

實·用·會·話·2

A : Hello. May I speak to Cathy, please?

B : Oh, just a minute, please. Cathy, it's for you.

C : Hello, this is Cathy speaking. Who is it, please?

A : Hi, Cathy, it's me, David. Listen, there is a very good film on in the local cinema. Would you like to go with me tonight?

C：What is the name of the film?

A：The Bridges of Madison County.

C：Ah, it's really a wonderful film. I'd love to go.

A：Good. I'll come and pick you up at six o'clock. The movie starts at six thirty.

C：All right. See you then.

- - - - - - - - - - -

A：喂，請讓凱西聽電話。

B：哦，請稍等。凱西，妳的電話。

（稍後）

C：喂，我是凱西，請問你是哪一位？

A：嗨，凱西，是我大衛啦！是這樣啦，本地電影院正在上映一部非常好的電影。妳今晚想跟我去嗎？

C：是什麼電影？

A：是《麥迪遜大橋》。

C：啊，真的是一部好電影，我想去。

A：太好了！六點鐘我來接妳。電影六點半開始。

C：好，到時候見囉！

深入分析

1. There is a film on in the local cinema.
有一部電影在本地戲院上映中。

There is... on 這裡的 on 是副詞，表示「（電影）放映、（戲劇）上演、（展覽）展出、（音樂）播放等」，例如：

⊙I looked over the TV Guide to see if there was any interesting program on.

我瀏覽《電視導報》，看看有沒有有趣的節目放映。

2. I'd love to. 我願意！
表示「樂意去做某事」，通常是回覆對方的邀約。若是不答應，則可以說：" I'd love to..., but I..." 表示「我很想去，但是我…因為…（所以不能去）」加以拒絕，例如：

A：Would you like to go for an outing with me?

B：I'd love to.

A：你想和我一起去郊遊嗎？

B：我很樂意去。

A：Would you like to see a movie with me?

B：I'd love to, but I have other planes.

A：你想和我一起去看電影嗎？

B：我很想去，但是我有其他計畫了。

實·用·會·話·3 •————————•

A：Sales Section.

B：Is Mrs. Brown in?

A：Speaking.

B：Oh, hello, Mrs. Brown. This is Peter speaking. How are you?

A：Just fine, thanks. What can I do for you?

B：Well, I was wondering if I could drop in for a few minutes today.

A：I'm a little busy today. Can you come right away?

B：I think I can make it in ten minutes or so.

A：Fine. I'll be expecting you.

B：Thanks, see you in a few minutes.

－－－－－－－－－－－－－－－－－

A：這是營業部。

B：布朗女士在嗎？

A：我就是。

B：哦，布朗女士，妳好。我是彼得，妳好嗎？

A：還好，謝謝。有何指教？

B：嗯，我在想今天否能去拜訪妳。

A：我今天有點忙。你能馬上過來嗎？

B：我想我十分鐘左右就可以到妳那裡。

A：好的。我等你。

B：多謝了。等會兒見。

深入分析

1. I was wondering if... 不知道（能否）……

是一種禮貌性的詢問語句，表示「不知道能否…」，例如：

⊙ I was wondering if you could spare me a few minutes.

不知道我能否耽擱你幾分鐘的時間？

2. drop in someone 拜訪某人

為動詞＋副詞結構的片語動詞，意思是「拜訪」，例如：

A：I just dropped in to say goodbye.

B：What time are you leaving?

A：我只是順道過來到別的。

B：你什麼時候要離開？

3. I can make it. 我能辦得到！

make it 這個片語具有廣泛的解釋，如「能做到、成功、完成等」，要視所要表達的實際狀況來決定其意思，例如：

⊙ They made it at last.

他們終於成功了。

⊙ Can you make it?

你做得到/趕得及嗎？

⊙ I can't make it in two months.

我無法在兩個月的時間內完成。

6
打電話

實·用·會·話·4

A：Hello?

B：Hello. May I speak to Mary, please?

A：Speaking.

B：Hi, Mary. This is Tom. I called to ask if you are busy tomorrow evening.

A：Let me see. No, I don't think I've got anything planned.

B：Well, I thought we might have dinner together and go to the movies.

A：Oh, that sounds like fun.

B：Good. I'll pick you up at 6:00 then.

A：Thanks! I'll see you tomorrow. Bye, Tom.

－－－－－－－－－－－－－－－

A：喂？

B：喂，請找瑪麗聽電話。

A：我就是。

B：嗨，瑪麗。我是湯姆。我打電話是要問明天晚上妳有沒有空。

A：我想想，我想我還沒有計畫要做什麼。有事嗎？

B：噢，我想我們可以共進晚餐，然後一起去看電影。

A：哦，聽起來很有趣。

B：太好了！那麼我六點來接妳。

A：謝謝，明天見。再見，湯姆。

深入分析 　　　　　　　　　　MP3 043

1. **That sounds like fun.** 聽起來很有趣。

　　當對方提出一個建議時，你覺得很有趣，就可以用常用片語 "sound+形容詞"，例如 "That sounds like fun." 若是在對方提出邀情的情境中，則表示你願意接受邀請的意思，例如：

　　A：Let's go fishing.

　　B：Sounds like great.

　　A：我們去釣魚吧！

　　B：聽起來不錯耶！

2. **I'll pick you up at six o'clock.** 我六點鐘來接你。

　　pick up 為動詞+副詞結構片語動詞，意思是「接（某人）」，例如：

　　⊙David comes to school to pick him up every day.

　　大衛每天來學校接他。

實·用·會·話·5

A：Hello?

B：Hello. May I speak to Kenny, please?

A：I'm sorry. He's not in right now. Who's calling, please?

B：This is Jim, his colleague.

A：Hi, Jim. Can I take a message?

B：Yes. Please ask him to call me back at 86473663.

A：Was that 86473663?

B：Yes.

A：OK. I'll give him the message. Goodbye, Jim.

B：Thank you. Goodbye.

- - - - - - - - - - - - - - - - -

A：喂？

B：喂，請找肯尼聽電話。

A：對不起，他現在不在。請問你是哪一位？

B：我是吉姆，他的同事。

A：嗨，吉姆。要不要我傳話？

B：好。請他回電到 86473663 找我。

A：是 86473663 嗎？

B：對。

A：好的。我會轉告他。再見！

B：謝謝。再見！

MP3 044

實·用·會·話·6

A：Hello. May I speak to Jenny, please?

B：Oh, just a minute, please. Jenny, it's for you.

(Later)

C：Hello, this is Jenny speaking. Who is it, please?

A：This is Tom speaking. Would you like to see a movie with me tonight?

C：What is the name of the film?

A：The Lord of The Ring.

C：Ah, it's really a wonderful film. I'd love to go.

－－－－－－－－－－－

A：喂，請找珍妮聽電話。

B：噢，請等一下。珍妮，找妳的。

（稍後）

C：喂，我是珍妮。請問你是哪一位？

A：我是湯姆。今天晚上妳想和我去看電影嗎？

C：什麼電影啊？

A：《魔戒首部曲》。

C：啊，確實是一部好電影。我要去。

6
打
電
話

深入分析

★**Would you like (to) ...?**　你想⋯⋯嗎？

這是一句非常口語的邀約用法，不論在正式
場合或一般生活場合都非常適用，帶有邀請
或詢問的意思，在 like 後面可以有兩種搭
配方式，一種是 "like＋名詞" ，另一種則
是 "like＋to＋原形動詞" ，例如：

⊙ Would you like a cup of tea?
　你想來杯茶嗎？

⊙ Would you like to join us?
　你想加入我們嗎？

🎵 045

實·用·會·話·7

A：Hello?

B：Hello. May I speak to Mark, please?

A：Sure, just a minute. Mark, you're wanted on
　the phone.

(Later)

C：Hello, this is Mark speaking.

B：Hi! This is Kent. How come you didn't
　come in today?

C：Oh, we had a farewell party for David last
　night. As a matter of fact, I woke up with a
　terrible hangover.

B：That's too bad. You'll have to be more
　　careful next time.

－－－－－－－－－－－－－－－－

A：喂？

B：喂，請找馬克聽電話。

A：好啊，等一下。馬克，你的電話。

（稍後）

C：喂，我是馬克。

B：嗨！我是肯特。你今天怎麼沒來上班？

C：噢，昨晚我們為大衛舉行歡送會。事實上，
　　我醒來後發現有嚴重的宿醉。

B：真糟糕。下次你該小心點兒。

深入分析

★**How come you didn't come today?** 為什麼你今天沒來？

　　"How come..." 是個很口語化的說法，意思是詢問原因，相同的意思還有 why 的用法，若是否定式的疑問語句，則可以用 why not 表示，例如：

A：How come you didn't appear at the dancing party?

B：I don't wanna go with David.

A：Why not?

A：你為什麼沒有去參加舞會？

B：我不想和大衛一起去。

A：為什麼不想？

實·用·會·話·8

A：This is Mrs. Lee in Apt. 212. May I speak with the manager, please?

B：This is he.

A：I've a problem in my apartment. The faucets on my kitchen sink are stuck. I can't turn them off.

B：I'm getting ready to go home now. That doesn't seem like a big problem. Could you wait until tomorrow?

A：What do you mean it's not a big problem? What about the flood in my kitchen?

B：OK. I'll be up there right away.

━ ━ ━ ━ ━ ━ ━ ━ ━ ━ ━

A：我是 212 號公寓的李太太。我想找經理聽電話。

B：我就是。有什麼需要我服務的嗎？

A：我的公寓出了點問題。我廚房水槽的水龍頭卡住了。我沒有辦法把水關掉。

B：我現在已經準備好要回家了。看起來那不是什麼大問題。能等到明天嗎？

A：你說不是什麼大問題是什麼意思？那我廚房淹水怎麼辦？

B：好吧，我馬上就到。

深入分析

I can't turn them off. 我無法把他們關閉。

turn off/on 表示電器「關閉／打開電源」的
意思，若是門窗的關閉/打開，則要用 close/
open 表示，例如：

	the TV 開/關電視
⊙ turn off/on	the radio 開/關收音機
	the light 開/關燈
	the door 開/關門
	the window 開/關窗

🎵 047

實·用·會·話·9 ●

A：Good morning. Evans Company. May I help you?

B：Could I speak to Mr. Smith, please?

A：I'll see if he is available. Who shall I say is calling, please?

B：Bill Gordon.

A：Hold the line, please.

（Later）

A：Mr. Smith is in a meeting now. What can I do for you?

B：Well, I want to discuss with him the new contract we signed last week.

A：I don't think the meeting will go on much longer. Shall I ask him to call you when he is free?

B：Yes, that could be easiest.

A：Could I have your name again, please?

B：It's Bill Gordon.

A：And the number?

B：86473663. Thank you for your help. Goodbye.

A：You're welcome. Goodbye.

6 打電話

- - - - - - - - - - - - -

A：早安，這是埃文思公司，我能替你效勞嗎？

B：我能找史密斯先生嗎？

A：我去看看他是否有空。請問你是哪一位？

B：我是比爾‧戈登。

A：請稍候！

（稍後）

A：史密斯先生正在開會。我能幫什麼忙嗎？

B：噢，我想和他討論上週簽定的合約。

A：我想會議不會開得太久。他有空時再讓他回
　　電話給你好嗎？

B：好，那太好了。

A：請再告訴我你的大名好嗎？

B：我叫比爾‧戈登。

A：你的電話號碼是多少？

B：8647366。謝謝你幫忙，再見！

A：不客氣，再見！

Unit 7

談論天氣

★ What a lovely day.
　天氣真好！

★ The weather is terrible.
　天氣糟透了！

★ It's a perfect day for shopping.
　今天適合去購物。

★ It's a nice day.
　天氣真好。

★ It's an awful day.
　真是糟糕的一天。

★ It's very hot today.
　今天非常熱！

★ It's warm.
　天氣暖和。

★ It's humid.
　天氣潮濕。

★ It's dry.
　天氣乾燥。

★ It's foggy.
　起霧了。

★ It's snowing.
　下雪了。

- ★ It's raining now.
  現正在下雨。

- ★ It's cold.
  天氣很冷。

- ★ It's chilly.
  冷颼颼的。

- ★ It's a bit cloudy.
  今天有點多雲的。

- ★ It's freezing today.
  今天冷死了。

- ★ It's bitterly cold today.
  今天特別冷。

- ★ It's snowing heavily.
  雪下得很大。

- ★ It's windy this afternoon.
  下午風很大。

- ★ It's rather windy today.
  今天風真大。

- ★ It'll clear up tomorrow.
  明天會晴天。

- ★ It'll clear up soon.
  很快就會放晴。

★ It's a little cloudy.
天氣有一點多雲。

★ It's getting cloudy.
雲越來越多了。

★ It'll be a wet day, I'm afraid.
恐怕會下雨。

★ Is it going to rain today?
今天會下雨嗎？

★ It's going to rain soon.
很快就會下雨。

★ It's only a shower.
只是小雨。

★ It's getting warmer day by day.
天氣越來越暖和了。

★ Spring is my favorite season.
春天是我最喜歡的季節。

★ It's already spring.
已經是春天了。

★ Spring is almost over.
春天快結束了。

★ How is the weather today?
今天天氣如何？

★ What will the weather be like tomorrow?
明天天氣會怎麼樣？

★ What does the weather forecast say?
天氣預報怎麼説？

★ What's the weather forecast for tomorrow?
氣象預報説明天的天氣如何？

★ What's the temperature today?
今天的溫度是多少？

★ The temperature has climbed to 36 ℃.
溫度已經上升到了攝氏36度。

MP3 050

實·用·會·話·1

A：What a lovely day!
B：Yes, isn't it?
A：Do you think it will also be the same
　　tomorrow?
B：I hope so. But the weather is changeable in
　　spring here. So when you go out, you'd
　　better take an umbrella with you.

— — — — — — — — — — — —

A：天氣真好呀！
B：可不是嗎？
A：你覺得明天天氣也會一樣好嗎？

B：希望是這樣吧，但在這裡的春天氣候是多變
　　的，所以你外出時，最好帶著雨傘。

實·用·會·話·2 ●

A：A beautiful day, isn't it?

B：Yes. Nice and sunny for a change.

A：It's so great to see sunshine again after tho-
　　se rainy days.

B：I prefer sunny days to rainy days.

— — — — — — — — — — — — —

A：多好的天氣，對嗎？

B：是呀，總算是風和日麗了。

A：下了這麼多天的雨之後再見到陽光，
　　真是太好了。

B：我喜歡和煦的日子，不太喜歡下雨的日子。

深入分析

prefer A to B　比起 B 來，更喜歡 A

通常是指和後者（B）比起來，較喜歡前者（A），例如：

⊙I prefer tea to coffee.

　茶和咖啡比起來，我更喜歡前者。

另外，若是以動作相比所作出選擇，則用 "prefer to do... than do..." 句型，例如：

⊙I prefer to stay at home than go to watch the film.

　我寧願待在家裡也不願去看電影。

 051

A : I wonder what the weather will be like tomorrow.

B : I haven't heard the weather report on the radio. But I expect it will be warm, too.

A : I think so. It seems days are getting longer and longer.

B : Yes. Summer is around the corner.

A : Many people, especially the young people, are looking forward to its coming.

B : Right. It is a season of sports.

7
談論天氣

A：不知道明天的天氣會怎麼樣。

B：我沒有聽到收音機播報的天氣預報，但我希
望天氣會變溫暖。

A：我也這樣想。看起來白天的時間變得越來越
長了。

B：是啊，夏天快要到了。

A：我想很多人，特別是年輕人都盼望夏天的來
臨。

B：對，那是運動的季節。

深入分析

★**Summer is around the corner.**
夏天就快來了。

　　"around the corner" 字面意思是「在角
落」，引申為空間或時間上的「在附近、將
來臨」的意思，例如：

A：Where is he?

B：He is just around the corner.

A：他在哪兒？

B：他就在附近。

⊙Christmas is around the corner!!
聖誕節快到了！

052

實·用·會·話·4 ●

A：I'm afraid we'll have a very hot summer this year. I don't know where to go for my summer vacation.

B：Why don't you go to the countryside? The weather will be cooler there.

A：Good idea! Do you often spend summer holidays in the mountains?

B：Yes. I enjoy cooler weather and I can visit my grandparents.

A：我們今年恐怕會有一個酷熱的夏季。我不知道要去哪裡過暑假。

B：為什麼不到鄉下去呢？那裡的天氣比較涼快。

A：好主意！你經常去山上度暑假嗎？

B：是的，我可以享受涼快的夏天，而且還能探望我的祖父母。

實 用 會 話 5

A：It looks like it's going to be sunny.

B：Yes, it's much better than yesterday.

A：But it's supposed to get cloudy and windy again this afternoon.

B：Well, the worst of the winter should be over.

─ ─ ─ ─ ─ ─ ─ ─ ─ ─ ─ ─ ─ ─

A：天氣好像會變晴！

B：是啊，天氣比昨天好多了！

A：但是今天下午可能又會變起風陰天。

B：嗯，最糟糕的冬天應該快過去了！

MP3 053

實 用 會 話 6

A：Beautiful day, isn't it?

B：Yes, it's not like what the radio said at all.

A：I wish it would stay this way for the weekend.

B：As long as it doesn't snow.

A：That's right. I've got to go now.

B：Sure. I'll see you back at home.

─ ─ ─ ─ ─ ─ ─ ─ ─ ─ ─ ─ ─ ─

A：天氣真好，對吧？

B：是啊，沒有像廣播說的那樣。

A：希望一直到週末都是這樣。

A：沒錯！我要走囉！

B：好，家裡見囉！

深入分析

1. at all 完全地

"at all" 是副詞片語，有極致化的表示，表示「非常地」、「完全地」、「徹底地」的意思，經常使用在否定的情境中，只要搭配上 not 即可，例如：

A：Are you busy now?

B：No, not at all. Why?

A：你現在忙嗎？

B：完全不會啊！有什麼事？

A：What happened?

B：I don't know at all.

A：發生什麼事了？

B：我完全不知道！

2. as long as 只要

表示條件式的說明，通常是假設性的情境，例如：

⊙ You can have a dog as long as you promise to take care of it.

只要你答應好好照顧，就可以養狗。

7 談論天氣

日期與時間

詢問日期或時間

★ What is today's date?
今天是幾月幾號？

★ What date is it today?
今天是幾月幾號？

★ What's the date today?
今天是幾月幾號？

★ What day is it?
今天是星期幾？

★ What time is it now?
現在幾點了？

★ What's the time?
幾點了？

★ Do you have the time?
你知道現在幾點了嗎？

★ Have you got the time?
你知道幾點了嗎？

★ Could you tell me the time?
你能告訴我幾點了嗎？

★ May I ask the time?
請問現在幾點了？

★ Is your watch right?
你的錶準嗎？

★ Does your watch keep good time?
你的錶時間準確嗎？

★ Isn't your watch a bit fast?
你的錶是不是有點快？

★ My watch seems to be slow.
我的錶好像慢了。

★ Mine seems to be fast.
我的(時間)好像快了。

 055

說明日期與時間

★ It's May first.
(今天)是五月一日。

★ It's the fifteenth of January.
(今天)是一月十五日。

★ It's Sunday.
(今天)是天星期天。

★ It's half past nine.
(現在)是九點半。

★ It's fifteen after three.
(現在)是三點十五分。

★ It's seven o'clock sharp.
(現在)是七點整。

★ It's exactly ten o'clock. I just heard the signal.
(現在)是十點整。我剛聽到鐘響。

★ It's a quarter to eleven.
(現在)差十五分就十一點了。

★ It's ten after two.
(現在)是兩點十分。

★ It's eight forty-five.
(現在)是八點四十五分。

★ It's midday.
(現在)是十二點。

★ It's almost noon.
(現在)快要中午了。

★ It's mid-night.
(現在)是午夜十二點。

★ It's eleven forty a.m.
(現在)是上午十一點四十分。

★ It's one forty p.m.
  (現在)是下午一點四十分。

★ It's sixteen hundred hours Taipei Time.
  (現在)是台北時間十六點鐘。

★ It's twenty-one hundred hours GMT.
  (現在)是格林威治時間二十一點鐘。

★ My watch says it's six o'clock.
  我的手錶現在是六點鐘。

★ It keeps good time.
  這錶走得很準。

★ It gains thirty seconds a day.
  它每天快三十秒。

★ It loses about two minutes a day.
  它每天慢兩分鐘。

★ It's ten minutes slow.　　　　　　🎵 056
  慢十分鐘。

★ It's ten minutes fast.
  快十分鐘。

★ It loses a bit.
  它有點慢。

特定時間

★ Time is up.
時間到了。

★ No more time.
沒時間了。

★ Time to go home.
回家的時間到了。

★ Time to say goodbye.
該說再見了。

★ Time for bed.
上床的時間到了。

★ It's about time to leave.
該離開的時間到了。

★ Now is the time to fight back.
該是反擊的時候了。

★ It's about time for my departure.
我該離境的時間到了。

★ I have plenty of time.
我的時間還很多。

★ I have no time.
我沒時間。

MP3 057

★ I don't have any time.
  我沒有時間。

★ I have no time for novels.
  我沒有時間看小說。

★ You are wasting my time.
  你在浪費我的時間。

★ The plane is timed to arrive at five.
  飛機訂於五點鐘抵達。

★ It's on time.
  準時。

★ It's in time.
  即時。

★ It's late.
  遲到了。

★ It's early.
  還很早。

★ How much time can you get?
  你有多少時間？

★ How much time is left?
  還剩下多少時間？

★ How much time is spent in each activity?
  每個活動花了多少時間？

A：Mary, have you got the time?

B：Yes, it's nine twenty.

A：Is your watch right?

B：I think so. I set it by the radio this morning.

A：How time flies! Let's call it a day.

A：瑪麗，妳知道現在幾點了嗎？

B：知道，九點廿分了。

A：妳的錶準嗎？

B：我想是的。今天早上我有用收音機校正時間。

A：時間過得真快呀！今天就到這裡吧！

深入分析

★**Let's call it a day.** 我們今天就到此為止吧！

字面意思是「稱為一天」，表示「現在可以結束目前手頭上在忙的事」。

實·用·會·話·2

A：What's the time, David?

B：My watch says seven o'clock.

A：Does your watch keep good time?

B：Yes, it keeps very good time. It's one of those new digital watches, which are very reliable. One small battery keeps it running accurately for at least a year.

A：That's very convenient. I hope I have one like yours.

B：But yours is nice, too.

A：It was, but it gains six minutes a day recently. I've got to have it repaired.

— — — — — — — — — — — — — — —

A：大衛，幾點了？

B：我的手錶是七點鐘。

A：你的手錶有準嗎？

B：有啊，很準啊！這是幾種不錯的新型電子錶之一。一個小號電池可以用上至少一年。

A：那到是挺方便的。我希望也有一支你那樣的錶。

B：你的錶也不錯呀！

A：以前還可以。但最近每天快六分鐘，得去送修了。

深入分析

1. keep good time 時間很準

若是說明鐘錶的「時間很準時」通常會使用 "keep good time"，記住不可以在 good 前面加冠詞 a，因為時間是不可數的。另外，若是表示「準時」，則可以用片語 "on time"，例如：

A：Are you coming?

B：Sure. I'll be there on time.

A：你有要來嗎？

B：會啊，我會準時到。

2. gain six minutes a day 每天快六分鐘

若是鐘錶時間是有慣性的變快，則表示時間的「增加」，那麼就是可以用 gain（增加）表示，反之，若是「變慢」，則是「減少」的概念，可以用 lose（損失）來說明，例如：

A：My watch gains five minutes a day. How about yours?

B：Mine loses ten minutes every day.

A：我的手錶一天會快五分鐘。你呢？

B：我的每天慢十分鐘。

實·用·會·話·3 ●

A：Excuse me, could you tell me the time?

B：Yes, it's five to eight by my watch.

A：What's the time you use here?

B：We are on Taipei Time. It's the standard time for the whole country.

A：What's the difference between your time and GMT?

B：There's a difference of eight hours. When it is nine o'clock in the morning in London, it's five o'clock in the afternoon of the same day here.

A：Oh, I see. When people in my country have just begun the day's work, people here are ready to get off work.

B：That's right.

- - - - - - - - - - - - - - - - -

A：對不起，你能告訴我現在的時間嗎？

B：好的，我的錶顯示還有五分就八點鐘了。

A：你們這裡採用什麼時間？

B：我們採用台北時間，這是全國的標準時間。

A：台北時間和格林威治時間有什麼區別？

B：八小時之差。當倫敦是早上九點鐘的時候，
　　這裡是同一天的下午五點鐘。

A：哦，明白了。當我們國家的人們剛剛要開始
　　一天的工作，這裡的人們正準備要下班。

B：沒錯！

深入分析

1. **GMT 格林威治時間**
   GMT 是 "Greenwich Mean Time" 的縮寫形
   式。

2. **get off work 下班**
   get off work 是指「下班」的意思，而不是
   out of work，千萬不要誤用喔，例如：
   A：When do you get off work?
   B：I usually get off at 5 pm.
   A：你什麼時候下班的？
   B：我通常在下午五點鐘下班。

實·用·會·話·4

A：Excuse me, do you have the time?

B：Sorry, I don't have my watch with me.

A：Thanks anyway.

- - - - - - - - - - - - - - - -

A：對不起，請問幾點了？

B：抱歉，我沒有帶錶。

A：還是謝謝你。

實·用·會·話·5

A：What time does your train leave?

B：At 12:30 pm.

A：Then we still have plenty of time.

- - - - - - - - - - - - - - - -

A：你乘坐的火車幾點鐘發車？

B：中午十二點半。

A：那麼我們還有很多時間。

實·用·會·話·6

A：What time do you usually get up?

B：At half past six, except on Saturdays and Sundays when I get up an hour later.

A：And when do you have your meals?

B：I have breakfast at seven, lunch at twelve, and dinner at six in the evening.

- - - - - - - - - - - - - -

A：你通常幾點鐘起床？

B：六點半，但星期六、星期天會多睡一個小時。

A：那麼是幾點鐘吃飯？

B：早餐是七點鐘，午餐則是十二點鐘，晚餐則是晚上六點鐘。

關心健康

說明身體狀況

★ I can't eat.
　我吃不下。

★ I can't sleep.
　我睡不著。

★ I can't stop coughing.
　我一直咳嗽。

★ I can't stop sneezing.
　我一直打噴嚏。

★ I can't stop shivering.
　我一直打顫。

★ I don't feel well.
　我覺得不舒服。

★ I'm not feeling well.
　我覺得不舒服。

★ I have a cold.
　我感冒了。

★ I have a bad cold.
　我得了重感冒。

★ I have a fever.
　我發燒了。

★ I have a headache.
我頭痛。

★ I have a ringing in my ears.
我耳鳴。

★ I have a runny nose.
我流鼻水！

★ I have a stuffy nose.
我鼻子不通。

★ I have a toothache.
我牙痛。

★ I have a cavity.
我蛀牙。

★ I have a sore throat.
我喉嚨痛。

★ I have a canker sore.
我嘴破。

★ I have a hiccup.
我打嗝。

★ I have stiff shoulders.
我肩膀痠痛。

★ I have a stomachache.
我胃痛。

★ I have diarrhea.
我拉肚子。

★ I have a chill.
我在打顫。

★ I feel dizzy.
我覺得頭暈。

★ I feel painful.
我覺得痛。

★ I feel tired.
我覺得累。

★ I feel dull.
我覺得頭昏。

★ I feel sick.
我感覺不舒服。

★ I feel like throwing up.
我想要吐。

★ I feel much better.
我覺得好多了。

★ I don't have any appetite.
我沒有食慾。

★ I can't breathe well.
我呼吸不順。

★ I'm constipated.
我便秘。

★ I'm injured.
我扭傷了。

★ I sprained my neck.
我扭傷脖子了。

★ I sprained my finger.
我扭傷手指了。

★ I sprained my ankle.
我扭傷腳踝了。

★ I broke my leg.
我摔斷腿了。

★ I ache all over.
我渾身痠痛。

★ My head hurts.
我頭痛。

★ My foot is killing me.
我的腳痛死了。

★ My heart is pounding.
我心跳得很厲害。

★ It hurts.
好痛！

★ It's bleeding.
流血了。

★ She passed out.
她暈過去了。

★ I need to see a doctor.
我需要看醫生。

★ I would like to see a doctor.
我需要看醫生。

★ Could you call an ambulance?
你可以叫救護車嗎？

詢問對方的狀況

★ You look terrible.
你看起來臉色糟透了！

★ You look pale.
你看起來臉色蒼白。

★ You don't look very well.
你的狀況看起來不太好。

★ Do you need any help?
你需要幫助嗎？

★ Do you need a doctor?
你需要看醫生嗎？

★ Do you want me to call an ambulance?
需要我叫救護車嗎？

★ What's wrong with you?
你有什麼問題嗎？

★ What are your symptoms?
你的症狀是什麼？

❾
關心健康

★ How are you today?
你今天怎麼樣？

★ How do you feel now?
你現在覺得如何？

★ What did you eat last night?　　　　MP3 064
你昨晚吃了什麼？

★ Let me check your blood pressure.
讓我量你的血壓。

★ How's your mother been?
你媽媽還好嗎？

★ Tell him I hope he's better soon.
轉告他希望他快一點復原。

★ Tell her I was asking about her.
轉告她我的問候。

★ Tell him not to work so hard.
　轉告他不要工作太累！

★ That's too bad. What does he have?
　太糟了！他生什麼病？

實·用·會·話·1

A：Hello, George. You look rather pale today.
　　Are you OK?
B：I'm staying home from work.
A：What's wrong?
B：It's a bad cold.
A：I hope you'll get over it soon.

- - - - - - - - - - - - - - - -

A：你好，喬治。你今天看起來臉色很蒼白。你
　　沒事吧？
B：我正休假在家。
A：怎麼了？
B：我重感冒了！
A：希望你早日康復。

★look＋形容詞　看起來…

"look＋形容詞" 的片語，形容從外表觀察得到某人的身體或精神狀況，例如：

A：You look gorgeous.

B：You think so? Thanks.

A：你看起來很漂亮。

B：你真的這麼想嗎？謝謝！

MP3 065

實·用·會·話·**2**

A：Hi, Mary. How are you today?

B：I'm not feeling well today.

A：Where are you going now?

B：As a matter of fact, I'm going to see the doctor.

A：What's the matter?

B：I've got a sore throat. It gives me so much pain that I can hardly eat.

A：Feel better soon.

━━━━━━━━━━━━━━━━━━

A：嗨，瑪麗。妳好嗎？

B：我今天感覺不好。

A：妳現在要去哪裡？

B：實際上，我要去看醫生。

⑨ 關心健康

A：怎麼了？

B：我喉嚨痛。疼得我幾乎吃不下飯。

A：祝妳早日康復。

實·用·會·話·3

A：How are you feeling today? Are you all right?

B：I'm OK, except that I've got a bad cough.

A：Oh dear, I'm sorry to hear that. How did it happen?

B：I was caught in the rain yesterday and ran a fever during the night. I took some aspirin, and when I woke up this morning, the fever was gone; but I started to cough.

A：Why don't you get some cough syrup? If it gets worse, you should see your doctor.

B：Yes, I will.

━ ━ ━ ━ ━ ━ ━ ━ ━ ━ ━ ━ ━ ━

A：你今天感覺怎麼樣？還好吧？

B：還好，只是一直咳嗽。

A：哦，聽你這麼說，我很難過。怎麼搞的？

B：昨天我淋了雨，夜裡就發燒了。我吃了一些阿司匹靈，早上醒來，燒退了，但是我開始咳嗽。

A：你可以喝些止咳糖漿。再不好的話，你就應
　　該去看醫生。

B：好，我會的。

　066

關心健康

1. be caught in the rain　被雨淋
caught 是 catch 的過去式。
catch 雖然是「抓住」、「逮捕」的意思，
但也可以解釋為「感染到疾病」的意思，
例如：
A：Are you OK? You look rather pale.
B：I must have caught the disease from him.
A：你還好吧？你看起來臉色蒼白。
B：我一定是被他傳染生病了。

2. I took some aspirin. 我吃了一些阿司匹靈。
took 是 take 的過去式。在英文中，「吃藥」
不是用吃 eat 這個單字，而是使用 take，例
如：
A：Why don't you take the medicine?
B：I did.
A：你怎麼不吃藥？
B：我吃了！

實·用·會·話·4

A：How's your dad coming along after the operation on his eye?

B：He's recovered well. And he's now up and about again.

A：But he's staying home from work, isn't he?

B：Yes. The doctor told him not to move too much and to have plenty of rest. On top of that he should not do any reading for the time being.

A：That's perhaps the last piece of advice he would like to follow.

B：Absolutely. And that's why he's feeling a little upset lately.

A：I hope he'll take it easy and feel like himself soon.

B：He will be glad to hear that you asked after him.

- - - - - - - - - - - - - - -

A：你爸爸眼部手術後恢復得怎麼樣？

B：恢復得很好。現在已經能起床四處走動了。

A：但他現在家休養，沒去上班，是吧？

B：對，醫生告訴他要少活動，多休息。
最重要的是目前不應該閱讀任何東西。

A：那恐怕是他最不願意聽從的忠告。

B：對極了。這就是為什麼他最近有點煩躁。

A：希望他放輕鬆點，一切都會轉好。

B：他會非常高興你在關心他。

深入分析

MP3 067

⑨ 關心健康

1. up and about　起來四處走動

是副詞片語，通常用來指病後恢復健康的人的活動狀況，表示無目的地走動。

2. feel like himself　感覺自如、完全恢復

feel like himself 字面意思「感覺像是他自己」，表示覺得很自在、舒服的意思，若使用在說明健康狀況，則是表示那個人的健康狀況良好的意思。

⊙It was not long before he felt like himself again.

不久他就完全恢復了。

實·用·會·話·5

A：I haven't seen Bob lately. How is he?

B：As a matter of fact, he's still pretty sick.

A：Oh, dear! What's up with him?

B：We don't know. He's going to see the doctor tomorrow.

A：Let me know if there's anything I can do.

B：Thank you very much. I'll tell him.

A：我最近都沒有見到鮑勃。他好嗎？

B：說實在的，他病得很嚴重！

A：哦，天哪！他得了什麼病？

B：我們不知道。他明天要去看醫生。

A：如果有什麼我能幫忙的，請告訴我。

B：非常感謝。我會告訴他的。

★as a matter of fact 事實上

表示還有事情未告知，而正打算說明時的暗
示性語法，類似這種「事實上…」的用法，
還有 "in fact, …" ，例如：

A：I suppose you haven't finished that report
　　yet?

B：I finished it yesterday, as a matter of fact.

A：我猜你還沒有完成那份報告？

B：事實上我昨天就完成了。

A：In fact, we both know it.

B：No, I wouldn't know.

A：事實上，我們都心知肚明！

B：沒有，我不知道！

❾
關
心
健
康

實·用·會·話·6

A：How is Jack been?

B：He's been out of work for a couple of days.

A：What's wrong with him?

B：He has a bad cold.

A：Well, tell him to take it easy and that I hope he feels better.

B：I'll tell him. Thanks for asking about him.

- - - - - - - - - - - - - -

A：傑克還好吧？

B：他好幾天沒有來工作了！

A：他怎麼了？

B：他得了重感冒。

A：是喔，告訴他好好休息，希望他快點好起來！

B：我會告訴他的，謝謝你關心他。

談喜好厭惡

問興趣

★ Do you have any hobbies?
你有什麼嗜好嗎？

★ What are your hobbies?
你的嗜好是什麼？

★ What are you interested in?
你對什麼有興趣？

★ What types of things do you want to try?
你想嘗試哪方面的事物？

★ What kind of books do you read?
你都看哪些書呢？

★ What kind of sports do you like?
你喜歡哪些運動呢？

★ What sort of music do you like?
你喜歡哪些類型的音樂？

★ What kind of book do you like?
你喜歡哪些類型的書？

★ What books do you like to read about?
你喜歡讀麼書？

★ What's your favorite sport?
你最喜歡什麼運動？

★ What sports do you like to play?
你喜歡什麼運動？

★ What do you think about this movie?
你覺得這部電影怎麼樣？

★ What do you think of this book?
你覺得這本書怎麼樣？

★ Who's your favorite singer?
你最喜歡的歌手是誰？

★ What's your favorite TV program?
你喜歡哪個電視節目？

★ What do you usually do during weekends?
週末你通常都做些什麼事？

★ How many books do you read a month?
你每個月看多少書？

★ How many movies do you see a year?
你一年看幾部電影？

★ Do you like playing chess?
你喜歡下棋嗎？

★ Do you like going to the movies?
你喜歡去看電影嗎？

★ Do you listen to the music at home?
你在家會聽音樂嗎？

★ Do you work out?
你有在健身嗎？

★ Are you good at singing?
你很會唱歌嗎？

★ Are you interested in gardening?
你對園藝有興趣嗎？

★ Are you good at dancing?
你擅長跳舞嗎？

說明興趣

★ I like it very much.
我非常喜歡這件事。

★ I'm crazy about it.
我對此很著迷。

★ I'm very interested in it.
我對此很感興趣。

★ It's OK.
還好。

★ It's not bad.
還不錯。

★ I don't like it.
我不喜歡。

★ I hate it.
我討厭它。

★ I have a strong dislike for it.
我很不喜歡。

★ I can't stand it.
我無法容忍。

★ I have a lot of interests.
我的興趣廣泛。

★ My only hobby is reading.　　　MP3 071
我唯一的興趣是閱讀。

★ Reading is my hobby.
閱讀是我的興趣。

★ Traveling is one of my favorite hobbies.
旅行是我最喜歡的興趣之一。

★ I'm good at dancing.
我擅長跳舞。

★ I'm very interested in music.
我對音樂很有興趣。

★ I'm interested in reading novels.
我喜歡讀小說。

★ I'm interested in the Internet.
我對網路很有興趣。

★ I'm very interested in photography.
我對攝影很有興趣。

★ I'm crazy about music.
我熱愛音樂。

★ I'm crazy about football.
我對足球很瘋狂。

★ I'm a drama fan.
我是個戲劇迷。

★ I'm taking dancing lessons.
我正在學跳舞。

★ I like bowling.
我喜歡打保齡球。

★ I like playing chess.
我喜歡下棋。

★ I like watching quiz shows on TV.
我喜歡看電視的猜謎節目。

★ I like listening to classical music.
我喜歡聽古典音樂。

★ I like listening to pop music on FM.
我喜歡聽調頻電台的流行音樂。

★ I like listening to Enya's songs.
我喜歡聽恩雅的歌。

★ I like to play golf.
我喜歡打高爾夫。

★ I like to read romantic novels.
我喜歡讀浪漫小說。

★ I like to go to museums during vacation.
我喜歡在假日去逛博物館。

★ I love to go shopping.
我喜歡去購物。

★ I love to play guitar.　　　　　MP3 072
我喜歡彈吉他。

★ I enjoy collecting stamps.
我喜歡集郵。

★ I enjoy listening to the music.
我喜歡聽音樂。

★ I enjoy listening to the music on holidays.
我喜歡在假日聽音樂。

★ I enjoy netsurfing almost every night.
我幾乎每天晚上都沈迷在上網。

★ I really enjoy soccer.
我真的很喜歡足球。

★ I play the guitar.
我會彈吉他。

★ I can play the guitar a little.
我稍微會一點吉他。

★ I think the film is wonderful.
我認為這部電影很棒。

★ I admire Cely Dion.
我很景仰席林‧迪翁。

★ I read mysteries as a pastime.
我的嗜好是看神秘小說。

★ I go to dancing classes three times a month.
我每個月上三次跳舞課。

★ I often read a book before going to bed.
我常在睡前看書。

★ I often enjoy video games at home.
我喜歡在家打電動。

★ I often browse in bookstores.
我常在書店裡隨便瀏覽。

★ I often watch TV after taking a bath.
我常在洗澡後看電視

★ I usually go to a pub on weekends.
我週末通常會去酒吧。

★ I usually spend time with my family.
我常在週末的時候陪伴家人。

★ I sometimes go to rock concerts.
我有時會去聽搖滾樂演唱會。

★ I sometimes spend all day on the Internet.
我經常整天上網。

★ I usually read novels when I have free time.
當我有空的時候，我經常讀小說。

★ I always borrow books from the library.
我常到圖書館借書。

★ I'd like to jog if I have time   **MP3** 073
如果有時間，我會去慢跑。

★ I'd rather stay home and watch TV all day long.
我寧願一整天待在家裡看電視。

★ I have been playing the piano since I was eight.
我從八歲的時候就開始彈鋼琴。

★ I haven't been to the movie theaters lately.
最近我都沒去電影院了。

★ I have no interest in sports.
我對運動沒什麼興趣。

★ I'm poor at dancing.
　我很不會跳舞。

★ I'm poor at singing.
　我很不會唱歌。

★ I've never played tennis.
　我沒有打過網球。

★ I was deeply moved by Miss Potter.
　《波特小姐》讓我很感動。

★ I was disappointed with Miss Potter.
　我對《波特小姐》感到失望。

★ One of my favorites book is Gone with the wind.
　我最愛的書籍之一是《亂世佳人》。

★ Of all the moves stars, I like Tom Cruise the best.
　電影明星之中，我最喜歡湯姆‧克魯斯。

★ Roman Holiday is the best film I've ever seen.
　《羅馬假期》是我看過最棒的電影。

★ My favorite poet is Tim Washington.
　我最喜歡的詩人是提姆‧華盛頓。

★ My favorite actor is Harrison Ford.
我最喜歡的演員是哈里遜‧福特。

★ My favorite painter is Picasso.
我最喜歡的畫家是畢卡索。

★ My favorite composer is Mozart.
我最喜歡的作曲家是莫札特。

 074

實·用·會·話·1

A：Do you like tennis?
B：Yes, I do. I'm crazy about tennis.
A：Really? So am I. How about basketball?
B：I love basketball too. It's exciting.

－ － － － － － － － － － － － － － － － －

A：你喜歡打網球嗎？
B：喜歡。我非常喜歡網球。
A：真的嗎？我也是。籃球怎麼樣？
B：我也愛打籃球。很刺激！

❿
談喜好厭惡

深入分析

★be crazy about... 對⋯⋯著迷

"be/go crazy about" 表示對某種事物熱衷
的喜好，是一種幾近瘋狂的狂熱態度，例
如：

⊙He is crazy about football games.

他對足球運動非常著迷。

⊙Don't go crazy about computer games.

不要迷戀於電腦遊戲。

不單只是對事物的熱衷，"be crazy about"
也可以表示對人的一種迷戀心態，例如：

⊙David is crazy about that girl.

大衛瘋狂地愛上了那個女孩。

實·用·會·話·2

A：What's your favorite subject at school?

B：English, of course. It's interesting and useful.

A：When did you become interested in it? I thought you never liked languages.

B：Well, I don't like the Chinese class, too much classics and too much recitation. The English class is more fun.

— — — — — — — — — — — — — — — — —

A：你最喜歡什麼科目？

B：當然是英語。英語有趣而且有用。

A：你什麼時候開始對英語感興趣的？我以為你從來都不喜歡語言的。

B：哦，我不喜歡中文課，經典太多，背誦太多。英語課比較有趣。

 075

實·用·會·話·3

A：Great party, isn't it?

B：Yes, it is. The band is fantastic and so is the food.

A：By the way, my name is Bill.

B：I'm Helen.

A：Would you like a drink, a glass of beer?

B：No, thanks. I don't like beer that much.

A：Well, how about a glass of wine?

B：That sounds good.

A：Red or white?

B：White, please. And dry. I like dry white wine.

A：So do I. Waiter! Two glasses of white wine. Dry, please.

- - - - - - - - - - - - - - -

A：晚會棒極了，不是嗎？

B：是啊。樂隊棒極了，餐點也是（很棒）。

A：對了，我叫比爾。

B：我是海倫。

A：來杯飲料怎麼樣，要不要喝啤酒？

B：不，謝謝！我不太喜歡啤酒。

A：那麼來葡萄酒如何？

B：好啊！

A：紅葡萄酒還是白葡萄酒？

B：請來杯白葡萄酒吧，不甜的。我喜歡不甜的白葡萄酒。

A：我也是。侍者，請來兩杯白葡萄酒，要不含糖的。

by the way, ... 順帶一提

當你想要轉換話題或是突然想起某件事要先插話說明時，就可以利用 "by the way" 作為前提的提醒，類似中文的口語：「對了，…」，例如：

A：It's a great party, isn't it?

B：That's right.

A：By the way, I am David.

B：Tracy.

A：很棒的派對，不是嗎？

B：沒錯！

A：對了，我是大衛。

B：我是崔西。

⑩ 談喜好厭惡

實·用·會·話·4 •

A：Are you watching the TV series now shown on Channel 8?

B：No, I haven't been watching it. I don't care much for soap operas. They are just not my cup of tea.

A：They are too confusing. But a lot of people enjoy watching them. They say soaps are entertaining.

B：Yes, only two kinds of people like watching soap operas.

A：Who are they?

B：Those who don't have to work and those who have too much work. The former need something to help them kill time and the latter need something to take their minds off work.

A：You are exactly right.

— — — — — — — — — — — — —

A：你現在收看第八頻道的電視連續劇嗎？

B：我沒看。我不太喜歡肥皂劇，不合我的胃口。

A：這種劇太讓人糊塗了。但很多人卻喜歡看。他們說肥皂劇只是讓人用來消遣。

B：只有兩種人喜歡看肥皂劇。

A：哪些人呢？

B：那些沒有工作的和那些工作過度的。前者需要消磨時光，後者需要讓自己忘掉工作。

A：對極了。

深入分析

1. not my cup of tea　不對我的口味

表示「不是我所喜歡的」，和現在很流行的口語中文「不是我的菜」一樣，表示「不喜歡」，例如：

⊙Novels by J. K. Rowling are not my cup of tea.

J. K.羅琳寫的小說我不喜歡。

2. kill time　消磨時間

字面意思是「殺死時間」，引申為「消磨時間」、「打發時間」，例如：

⊙They played cards to kill the time.

他們打撲克牌消磨時間。

3. take one's minds off　放鬆

字面意思是「將思想抽離」，表示「放輕鬆」、「不要想太多」的意思，例如：

⊙I often listen to light music to take my mind off.

我常聽輕音樂來放鬆自己。

道 歉

道歉

★ Excuse me.
借過。╱對不起。╱打擾一下。

★ Will you excuse us?
我們失陪一下！

★ Sorry for being late.
對不起，我遲到了。

★ Excuse my interrupting you.
對不起，打擾你們。

★ Sorry for interrupting your talk.
抱歉打斷各位的談話。

★ Sorry.
抱歉。

★ I'm sorry.
抱歉。

★ I'm very sorry about that.
為此我很抱歉。

★ I'm terribly sorry.
我很抱歉。

★ I'm awfully sorry.
我很抱歉。

★ Sorry! Did I step on you?
抱歉，我是不是踩到你了？

★ Sorry, David, I have to cancel our meeting.
抱歉，大衛，我得取消我們的會議。

★ Sorry, I can't do it by myself.
抱歉，我沒有辦法自己一個人完成。

★ Sorry I can't stop. I have no time.
抱歉，我不能停下。我沒有時間。

★ Sorry, I didn't catch you.
抱歉，我沒有聽懂。

★ Sorry, I don't know.
抱歉，我不知道。

★ Sorry, I kept you waiting.
抱歉，讓你久等了。

★ I'm sorry to bother you.
對不起給你添麻煩了！

★ I'm sorry to bother you with all this work.
很抱歉麻煩你做這些事。

★ I'm sorry to disappoint you.
很抱歉讓你失望了。

★ I'm sorry to disturb you.
對不起，打擾你了。

★ I'm sorry to let you down.
對不起讓你失望了。

★ Pardon?
你說什麼？

★ I beg your pardon. I suppose I should have knocked.
抱歉，我想我應該先敲一下門的。

★ I apologized to you.
我向你道歉。

★ Please forgive me.
請原諒我。

★ Please accept my apology.
請接受我的道歉。

★ Will you forgive me?
你能原諒我嗎？

★ I'm sorry for what I have said to you.
我為我向你說過的話表示歉意。

★ I'm sorry. I didn't mean to hurt your feelings.
對不起。我沒有傷害你的意思。

★ I'm afraid I've brought you too much trouble.
我想我已經給你帶來太多的麻煩了。

對道歉的回覆

★ That's OK.
沒關係!

★ That's all right.
沒關係!

★ It's nothing.
沒什麼!

★ Never mind.
不要在意!

★ It doesn't matter.
不要緊!

★ It's no trouble at all.
一點也不麻煩的!

★ It's not your fault.
不是你的錯!

★ It's no big deal.
沒什麼大不了的!

★ Everything will be fine.
凡事都會順利的！

★ No problem.
沒關係啦！

★ Forget it.   🎧 079
算了！

★ Don't let it worry you.
別為此事擔心。

★ I quite understand.
我非常理解。

★ Never mind. It doesn't matter.
別介意！真的沒關係！

★ Please don't worry about that.
請別為此事擔心。

實·用·會·話·1

(B is taking to C)

A：Excuse me for interrupting.

B：Yes, what is it?

A：Would you please fill out this form? It's for our records.

B&C：No problem.

(Later)

A：Thank you. Sorry for the interruption.

C：That's all right.

- - - - - - - - - - - - - -

（B 和 C 正在說話）

A：對不起，打擾一下。

B：什麼事？

A：請你們填這張表格好嗎？這是我們存檔用
　的。

B&C：沒問題！

（稍後）

A：謝謝。對不起打斷了你們的談話。

C：沒關係！

深入分析

> ★**fill out** 填寫（表格）
>
> fill out 是個動詞片語，除了是「填寫（表
> 格）」之外，也有「長胖」的意思，例如：
> ⊙You'll have to fill out these forms before
> getting the loan.
> 核准貸款前，要填寫這些表格。
> ⊙Her cheeks have filled out.
> 她的臉頰豐腴起來了。

實·用·會·話·2

A：Excuse me, Mr. Smith. Would you please lend me your bike?

B：Certainly, here you are.

A：Thank you. I just want to go to the hospital.

B：There's no hurry. Take your time. I'm not using it now.

A：對不起，史密斯先生，可以把自行車借我用一下行嗎？

B：當然可以，（自行車）在這裡。

A：謝謝，我想去趟醫院。

B：別著急，慢慢來。我現在沒有要用。

深入分析

★**take your time　放鬆點**

字面意思是「拿你的時間」，卻也有「別著急」、「慢慢來」的意思，例如：

⊙Take your time, the meeting won't start till five.

別著急，會議五點鐘才開始呢！

實·用·會·話·3

A：Excuse me. Would you mind giving Miss Jones a message?

B：I'll be glad to.

A：Please tell her the computer class is not at seven thirty, but at seven tomorrow morning.

B：All right.

A：Thank you. And please don't forget.

B：No, I won't.

－ － － － － － － － － － － － － －

A：不好意思！你能幫我留話給瓊斯小姐嗎？

B：我很樂意！

A：請轉告她明早的電腦課是七點，而不是七點半。

B：好的。

A：謝謝！請別忘了(告訴她)。

B：不會，我不會忘記的。

深入分析

1. Would you mind...?　你介意…嗎？

這一句型用來表示客氣的請求，mind 表示
「介意…」，後接動名詞的形式，例如：

⊙ Would you mind passing me the salt?
能把鹽遞給我嗎？

2. I'll be glad to.　我很願意！

通常用來表達樂意幫助別人或去做某人所要
求的事，例如：

A：Would you help me with my English?

B：I'll be glad to.

A：你能幫我學英語嗎？

B：我很樂意（幫你）。

實·用·會·話·4

A：I'm terribly sorry, John. I lost your magazine.

B：It doesn't matter . It was a back number anyway.

A：I've tried to find another copy but couldn't find one.

B：Don't worry about it. I don't need it anymore.

—— —— —— —— —— —— —— —— —— —— ——

A：真是非常抱歉，約翰，我把你的雜誌弄丟了。

B：沒關係，反正是本過期雜誌。

A：我有想要再找一本，但沒能找到。

B：不用擔心，我也用不著它了。

⓫
道
歉

深入分析

I'm terribly sorry. 我非常地抱歉。

terribly 是副詞，表「非常地」的意思，程度比 very 更強烈，例如：

⊙I've been terribly worried about you all day.
　我一整天都非常地擔心你。

⊙We were terribly lucky to find you here.
　我們很幸運能在此找到你。

實·用·會·話·5

(On the phone)

A：Hello, Henry. It's Mary.

B：Hello, Mary. Good morning.

A：I'm very sorry, Henry. I'm not feeling well. I don't think I can go to the party tonight.

B：Oh, dear, I'm sorry to hear that.

A：I hope I'm not upsetting you too much.

B：Oh, well, I understand. Don't worry about the party.

- - - - - - - - - - - - - - - - -

（電話中）

A：喂，亨利，我是瑪麗。

B：喂，瑪麗，早安。

A：十分抱歉，亨利。我身體不太舒服。我看今晚的派對我無法參加了。

B：哎呀！這太遺憾了。

A：希望你不會失望。

B：噢，我能理解的。別為派對的事擔心了。

實·用·會·話·5

A：Would you like to go running?

B：I'd enjoy that. Where would you like to go?

A：We could go to the park. There shouldn't be many people there now.

B：Good. Just let me change.

A：Sure. Take your time.

————————————————

A：你要去跑步嗎？

B：我喜歡。你要去哪裡跑步？

A：我們可以去公園。現在不會有很多人。

B：太好了！我去換個衣服。

A：好！你慢慢來！

11
道
歉

★**I'd enjoy that.** 我很喜歡。

enjoy 後面的受詞只能用名詞、代名詞、反義代名詞和動名詞，不能用不定詞，例如：

listening to the music 喜歡聽音樂

⊙enjoy reading books 喜歡讀書

playing baseball 喜歡打棒球

以下為enjoy的常用片語：

⊙enjoy oneself 玩得開心

⊙enjoy one's holiday 假日玩得開心

實·用·會·話·6

A：Hi, Juliet.

B：Hi, David. Come on in. Coffee?

A：OK, thanks. Listen, let's go for a bike ride.

B：Sure. Where?

A：Let's call John and ask him. He always knows the best place to go.

B：That's a good idea. Just give me a few minutes to get ready.

━━━━━━━━━━━━━━━━━

A：嗨，茱莉亞。

B：嗨，大衛。進來吧，要喝咖啡嗎？

A：好，謝謝！是這樣的，我們一起去騎車吧！

B：好啊！去哪裡？

A：我們打電話給約翰問問他，他總是知道去哪裡是最好的。

B：好主意！給我幾分鐘的時間準備吧！

實·用·會·話·7

A：Hi, Betty. Busy now?

B：No, not at all.

A：Good. Do you want to go skiing with me?

B：I've never gone skiing.

A：Oh, come on. It's not hard. I'll show you how.

B：OK. I'll be ready in a minute.

━ ━ ━ ━ ━ ━ ━ ━ ━ ━ ━ ━

A：嗨，貝蒂！現在忙嗎？

B：不會，一點都不會！

A：太好了！你想要和我去滑雪嗎？

B：我沒有滑過雪耶！

A：喔，來吧，一點都不難。我教你！

B：好！我馬上好！

⑪
道
歉

in a minute 立即

"in a minute" 的字面意思是「在一分鐘內」，引申為「馬上」、「立即」的意思，例如：

A：Shall we?

B：I'll come in a minute.

A：可以走了嗎？

B：我馬上就來。

感 謝

表示感謝

★ Thanks.
多謝!

★ Thanks a lot.
多謝了!

★ Thank you.
謝謝!

★ Thank you very much.
非常感謝你!

★ Thank you so much.
非常感謝你!

★ Thank you anyway.
還是要感謝你!

★ Thanks to you and your staff.
謝謝你及你的員工!

★ Thank you for your help.
謝謝你的幫忙!

★ Thank you for your time.
感謝撥冗!

★ Thank you for your patience.
謝謝你的耐心!

★ Thank you for the delicious dishes.
感謝你的佳餚!

★ Thank you for everything.
所有的事都要謝謝你!

★ Thank you for all you have done for me.
謝謝你為我做的一切!

★ Thanks for your kindness.
謝謝你的好心!

★ Thanks for saying so.
感謝你這麼說!

★ Thanks for asking me out.
感謝你約我出來!

★ Thanks for cheering me up.
感謝你鼓勵我!

★ Thanks for asking.
謝謝(你的)邀請!

★ Thank you for coming.
謝謝你的來訪!

★ Thank you for calling.
謝謝你打電話!

★ Thank you for listening.
感謝你聽我傾訴!

12
感
謝

★ Thank you for telling me.
謝謝你告訴我！

★ Thank you for helping me.
謝謝你幫我！

★ Thank you for making me stronger.
感謝你讓我更強壯！

★ Thank you for making me feel important.
感謝你讓我覺得很重要！

★ Thank you for making me feel needed.
感謝你讓我覺得被需求！

★ Thank you for making me feel so loved.
感謝你讓我覺得被愛！

★ Thank you for making me feel confident.
感謝你讓我覺得有自信！

★ Thank you for making me feel so comfortable.
感謝你讓我覺得舒服自在！

★ Thank you for making me feel welcome and comfortable.
感謝你讓我覺得舒服自在和受歡迎！

★ Thank you for making me feel safe and wealthy.

感謝你讓我覺得安全及富裕!

★ Thank you for making me breakfast every morning.

感謝你每天幫我做早餐!

★ Thank you for making me become interested in English.

感謝你讓我變得對英文有興趣!

★ Thank you for making me so welcome here.

謝謝你讓我覺得在這裡是受歡迎的!

★ Thank you for making me calm down in time!

感謝你讓我及時冷靜下來!

★ Thank you for making me one of your members.

感謝你讓我成為你們的一員!

★ Thank you for letting me know I wasn't the only one.

感謝你讓我知道我不是孤獨的!

12
感
謝

★ Thank you for making me feel so special on my birthday.
感謝你讓我在我生日時感覺這麼特別！

★ Thank you for remembering my birthday.
感謝記得我的生日！

★ Much appreciated.
非常感激！

★ I appreciate your help.
感謝幫忙！

★ I appreciate your kindness.
感謝你的關心！

★ It's really helpful.　　　　　　**MP3** 086
很有幫助！

★ I really appreciate it.
我真的很感謝！

★ I can't thank you enough.
真不知道該如何感謝你！

★ I have no words to thank you.
不知道要說什麼才能感謝你！

★ You have been very helpful.
你真的幫了大忙！

★ That's very nice of you.
　你真好！

★ That's very kind of you.
　你真好！

★ How kind of you.
　你真好！

對謝意的回覆

★ You are welcome.
　不客氣！

★ It's OK.
　沒關係！

★ Not at all.
　完全不會！

★ No problem.
　一點也不（麻煩）。

★ Don't mention it.
　不客氣！

★ Don't worry about it.
　別這麼說！

★ It was no trouble.
不麻煩！

★ My pleasure.
我的榮幸！

★ You should.
你是應該（說謝謝）！

★ Sure.
當然（要說謝謝）。

 087

實·用·會·話·1

A：Would you help me move this box?

B：OK. Oh, this box is very heavy.

A：Yes, it is. Now, I have to wrap the box.

B：Let's put the box down on the table.

A：Fine. Get me a hammer.

B：Here you are.

A：Thanks. You've been really helpful.

B：No problem.

— — — — — — — — — — — — — — —

A：你幫我移動一下這個箱子，好嗎？

B：好的！哦，這箱子可真重。

A：是啊。現在我要把箱子封起來。

B：把箱子放在桌子上吧。

A：好。幫我拿個錘子，好嗎？

B：給你！

A：謝謝！你真的幫了大忙！

B：不客氣！

實·用·會·話·2

A：Would you mind helping me hang up this picture?

B：Of course not. I'll be glad to.

A：Hold it straight, while I put in the nail.

B：OK.

A：How does that look? Do I have it straight?

B：Yes, it's straight.

A：你介意幫我把這幅畫掛起來嗎？

B：當然願意效勞。

A：請把畫扶正。我要釘釘子。

B：好啊！

A：看看怎麼樣？掛正了嗎?

B：是的，掛正了。

深入分析

Of course not. 當然不。

因為問題是問 "Would you mind..."（你介意…嗎），所以回答 "Of course not" 表示「不介意做…」之意。

另一種 would you mind 的問句的回答方式，若表示願意，也可以說："No, not at all."（完全不介意），例如：

A：Would you mind closing the window for me?

B：No, not at all.

A：你介意幫我關窗戶嗎？

B：好，我不介意。

MP3 088

實·用·會·話·3

A：Oh, Jim. Would you do me a favor?

B：Why not.

A：Will you type this letter for me?

B：Certainly. When do you want it?

A：By tomorrow. Is it OK?

B：I think that will be all right.

A：Thank you very much.

B：Don't mention it.

A：噢，吉姆，幫我個忙，可以嗎？

B：當然可以啦！

A：能幫我把這封信打字好嗎？

B：當然可以。你什麼時候要？

A：明天之前，可以嗎？

B：我想可以吧！

A：那就太謝謝你啦！

B：不用客氣！

深入分析

Why not.　好啊！

這裡相當於 of course 或 OK，表示「願意、為何不」的肯定回答，而不是表示疑問。

A：Would you give me a hand?

B：Why not.

A：可以幫我忙嗎？

B：好啊！

實·用·會·話·4

A：Say, Henry, I was wondering if you could help me with my English.

B：My pleasure. When?

A：How about tomorrow afternoon?

B：I'm sorry, but I shall not be free then. What about this evening?

A：All right. This evening is fine. See you then. Thank!

B：Sure. See you.

— — — — — — — — — — — —

A：喂，亨利，你能不能輔導一下我的英語？

B：當然可以啦！什麼時候開始呢？

A：明天下午怎麼樣？

B：對不起，明天下午我沒空。今晚怎麼樣？

A：行，那就今晚吧！晚上見！謝謝！

B：不客氣！晚上見！

深入分析

1. I was wondering if... 是否可以⋯

雖然字面意思是「我在懷疑⋯」，但其實就是類似中文「我在想是否可以⋯」，是一種表示客氣或委婉的請求時的慣用語法，常用過去是 was 表示，很少會使用 "I'm wondering..."，例如：

A：I was wondering if you wanted to go with me.

B：No, I don't think so.

A：你要不要和我一起去？

B：不要！

2. How about...? 你覺得⋯如何？

和 "What about..." 一樣，都是用來表示向對方提出建議，意思是「⋯⋯可以嗎？」，例如：

⊙ How about the day after tomorrow?

後天行嗎？

3. be free 有空閒的

free 是形容詞「有空閒時間」的意思，但也表示「自由的」、「免費的」，例如：

⊙ When you buy a dinner for over \$10, you get a soda free.

晚餐超過十美元，就可以免費獲得汽水一杯。

請求幫助

尋求幫忙的要求

★ Give me hand, please.
請幫我一下。

★ I need help.
我需要幫助。

★ Help!
救命啊！

★ Can I ask a favor?
我可以要求幫忙嗎？

★ Can you...?
你能……嗎？

★ Would you do me a favor?
能幫我一個忙嗎？

★ Do me a favor and close the window, please.
請幫我個忙把窗戶關上。

★ I wonder if you could do me a favor.
不知道你能否幫我一個忙。

★ I was wondering if you could give me a hand.
不知你能不能幫我一個忙。

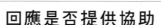

回應是否提供協助

★ Certainly.
當然。

★ Yes, of course.
好，當然可以。

★ OK.
好。

★ Sure. What is it?
好啊！（要幫）什麼？

★ What is it about?
是關於什麼事？

★ No problem.
沒問題！

★ Go ahead.
說吧，要幫什麼？

★ Leave it to me.
交給我來辦就好。

★ I'll do it for you.
我會幫你做。

★ What do you want me to do?
你要我做什麼？

13
請求幫助

★ I'll be happy to.
　我很樂意。

★ I'd be glad to.
　我很樂意去做。

★ I'd like to, but I have to go to the station right now.
　我倒是很想，但我必須馬上去一趟車站。

★ Sorry, I can't help you.
　抱歉，我不能幫你。

★ Sorry, I'm in the middle of something.
　抱歉，我正在忙。

★ I can't help you at the moment.
　我現在不能幫你。

★ I can't do anything now.
　我現在不能做任何事。

★ I have other business to take care of.
　我有事要忙。

★ Sorry, not right now.
　抱歉，現在不行。

★ Ask someone else.
　去要求別人吧！

★ I'm afraid I couldn't.
　我恐怕不行！

主動提供幫忙

★ Is there anything I can do for you?
  有什麼需要我幫你做的嗎？

★ Is there anything I can get for you?
  有什麼需要我幫你拿的嗎？

★ Is there anything I can buy for you?
  有什麼需要我幫你買的嗎？

★ Let me help you.
  我來幫你！

★ Let me give you a hand.
  我來幫你吧！

★ Would you like me to do it?
  你想讓我做嗎？

★ I can help you.
  我可以幫你。

★ Do you need help?
  你需要幫忙嗎？

★ How may I help you?
  有需要我幫忙的嗎？

接受對方的協助

★ It's very kind of you.
你真好。

★ Wouldn't that be too much bother?
那不是太麻煩你了嗎？

★ Please don't bother. Thank you all the same.
不麻煩你了！（但是）還是得謝謝你。

★ Please don't bother.
請不必這麼麻煩！

★ I can handle it by myself.
我可以自己來。

★ I can do it by myself.
我可以自己來。

★ I can manage it.
我可以自己來（不需要幫助）。

★ I can manage all right.
我可以自己來。

實·用·會·話·1

A：Hello, Tom. Would you do me a favor?

B：Sure.

A：Would you please mail this letter for me on your way to the bookstore?

B：Do you want it to be registered?

A：Yes, I think so. There are some pictures in it. It would be great pity if they were lost.

B：Yes. I will be glad to be of help.

A：Thanks.

B：Don't mention it.

＿ ＿ ＿ ＿ ＿ ＿ ＿ ＿ ＿ ＿ ＿ ＿ ＿ ＿

A：湯姆，你好。幫一個忙，好嗎？

B：你說吧！

A：你在去書店的路上幫我寄這封信，好嗎？

B：你想寄掛號信嗎？

A：是的，我是這樣認為。信裡有幾張照片。要是丟了，實在可惜。

B：好，我很樂意幫忙。

A：謝謝！

B：不客氣！

13 請求幫助

深入分析

1. do somebody a favor 幫某人的忙

favor 是「協助」的意思，do somebody a favor 是慣用語法，例如：

A：Please do me a favor and carry this luggage to the third floor.

B：No problem.

A：請幫我個忙，將行李搬到三樓。

B：沒問題！

2. Don't mention it. 別客氣！

字面意思是「不用提及」，是用來回答別人的感謝，意思是「別客氣」、「不用謝謝」。

A：Thank you for your help.

B：Don't mention it.

A：謝謝你的幫忙。

B：不用客氣！

實·用·會·話·2

A：Dude, busy now?

B：Not at all. What's up?

A：May I borrow your dictionary for a couple of days?

B：It depends on when.

A：Oh, just over the weekends. I won't keep it for long.

B：Yes, I guess that would be all right.

A：Thank you.

B：You're quite welcome.

— — — — — — — — — — — — — — —

A：兄弟，現在忙嗎？

B：不會啊！有事嗎？

A：我可以借你的詞典用幾天嗎？

B：看什麼時候要借。

A：噢，就這個週末。我不會借太久的。

B：好啊！我想可以。

A：謝謝！

B：不客氣！

深入分析

1. a couple of ...　好幾個…

和 several 一樣，意思是「幾個」而不是「一對」之意。

⊙ He went to Canada a couple of weeks ago.

　他幾週前去了加拿大。

但 a couple 單用時，則表示「一對（夫妻）」，例如：

⊙ They are a couple.

　他們是一對。

⊙ The young couple had a quarrel yesterday.

　年輕夫妻昨天吵了一架。

2. depend (on)...　取決於…

也可以在 depend 後面加 on+人/事/物，以說明足以做出決定的依據，例如：

A：Is there a meeting tomorrow?

B：It depends.

A：明天開會嗎？

B：不一定。

A：What do you say?

B：It depends on you.

A：你覺得呢？

B：由你決定！

實·用·會·話·3

A：Would you please do me a favor, David?

B：Of course. What is it?

A：Could you lend me your camera?

B：Sure, here you are.

A：Thanks. That's very kind of you.

― ― ― ― ― ― ― ― ― ― ―

A：大衛，幫個忙好嗎？

B：當然好。什麼事？

A：可以把相機借給我用嗎？

B：可以，給你。

A：謝謝！你真好。

實·用·會·話·4

A：Is there anything I can do to help you?

B：Yes, I'd like some help carrying these bags.

A：All right.

B：Thank you.

A：You're welcome.

― ― ― ― ― ― ― ― ― ― ―

A：有什麼事需要我幫忙的嗎？

B：有，我想請你幫我提一下這些手提包。

A：好的。

B：謝謝啦！

A：別客氣！

⑬ 請求幫助

實·用·會·話·5

A：Would you help me for a minute?

B：Yes. What do you want me to do?

A：Could you hold these packages while I look for the key to the door?

B：I'd be glad to.

- - - - - - - - - - - - - -

A：請問，你能幫我一會兒嗎？

B：好啊。你想要我做什麼？

A：你能幫我把這些包包拿著嗎？我來找一下門的鑰匙。

B：我很樂意。

深入分析

★**key to the door** 門的鑰匙

意思是「門的鑰匙」不是 key of the door。

這種表示所屬關係方法比較特殊，類似的表

達還有：

⊙ answer to the question

　問題的答案

⊙ entrance to the cinema

　戲院的門口

⊙ solution to the problem

　解決問題的方法

⊙ bridge to knowledge

　知識的橋

實·用·會·話·6

A：Oh, shit.

B：What's going on?

A：I've got a flat tire.

B：Are you in a hurry?

A：Yes. I have to go to the hospital to see David.

B：Get in. I can give you a lift.

A：That's very kind of you. Thank you very much.

B：You are welcome.

———————————————

A：喔，糟糕！

B：怎麼啦？

A：爆胎了。

B：你有急事嗎？

A：是的，我得去醫院看大衛。

B：上車，我送你一程。

A：你真是太好了。非常感謝。

B：別客氣！

實·用·會·話·7 ●

A：What's the matter with your foot?

B：I fell down the steps just now.

A：Let me have a look.

(A feels B's ankle.)

B：Ouch, that hurts.

A：Would you like me to take you to the
　　hospital? You might have broken a bone.

B：It's very kind of you. But David is getting a
　　car for me. Thank you just the same.

— — — — — — — — — — — — — — — —

A：你的腳怎麼啦？

B：我剛從樓梯上摔下來。

A：讓我看看。

（A 摸 B 的腳踝）

B：哎喲！好痛啊！

A：我帶你去醫院吧！你可能骨折了。

B：你真好，但大衛幫我叫車了，還是要謝謝
　　你。

13
請求幫助

深入分析

> ★**What's the matter with you?** 你怎麼啦？
>
> 和 "What's wrong?" 類似，是「出了什麼
> 問題？」，例如：
>
> ⊙ You look listless. What's the matter with
> you?
>
> 你看起來無精打采的，有什麼不舒服嗎？

實·用·會·話·8 ●──────────●

A : Let me help you with the suitcase, Alice.
Your hands are full.

B : I can manage all right, Henry. Thanks just
the same.

A : Come on, hand it over. It's pretty far to the
station.

B : Well, if you insist.

━ ━ ━ ━ ━ ━ ━ ━ ━ ━ ━ ━ ━ ━

A：艾麗絲，讓我來幫妳提箱子吧！妳手上拿的
東西太多了。

B：我自己能做到，亨利。儘管如此，還是要謝
謝你。

A：來吧，交給我吧。離火車站還相當遠呢！

B：好吧，假如你堅持一定要（幫我）的話。

深入分析

I can manage all right. 我能應付得了！

　　manage 表示「管理」，帶有「可以控制得很好」的意思，例如對方問你："Do you need help?"（是否需要幫忙？）若你自己可以處理，不需要對方的協助，就可以說："Thanks, I can manage."

⊙I can manage without his help.

　　沒有他的幫助，我也能應付得了。

同情

表達同情心

★ How unfortunate!
多不幸啊！

★ That's too bad!
太糟了！

★ That's a pity.
真可惜！

★ What a shame!
真可惜！

★ How sad to hear Tom's accident!
聽到湯姆的意外，真是令人悲傷！

★ What bad luck!
運氣真差！

★ I'm sorry to hear that.
聽到這件事我很難過。

★ I feel terribly sorry for you.
我為你感到難過。

★ I know how you must feel.
我理解你的感受。

回應對方的關心

★ Thank you.
謝謝你。

★ Thank you for asking.
謝謝關心。

★ Thank you so much for your concern.
非常感謝你的關心。

★ I appreciate your kindness.
我感謝你的好意。

★ It's very kind of you to help.
你來幫我真是太好了。

 098

實·用·會·話·1

A：I was told that Tom's house was robbed.

B：Yes. It happened last night.

A：How shocking! What did the robbers get away with?

B：Three thousand dollars in cash.

A：What a shame! Let's call him and see if we can be of any help.

A：我聽說湯姆的房子遭小偷了。

B：是的，昨天夜裡發生的。

A：太嚇人了！盜賊拿走了什麼？

B：三千元現金。

A：真可惜！我們打電話給他吧，看看能幫他做
　　點什麼。

深入分析

1. How shocking! 太嚇人了！

也可解釋為「真令人震驚」，表示說話者
的震驚，例如：

⊙ How shocking! He was murdered last night.
太嚇人了！他昨晚被謀殺了。

2. What a shame! 真可惜！

表示說話者的遺憾，例如：

⊙ What a shame! He hasn't passed the exam.
真可惜！他沒有通過這次考試。

實·用·會·話·2

A：Mary, I was really shocked to hear about your husband's accident!

B：We're just thankful that it wasn't any worse than it was.

A：Please let me know if there's anything I can do. I'll be glad to take care of the kids while you go to the hospital.

B：Thank you so much, Jenny. I might need your help tomorrow if you don't mind.

A：Not at all. And please tell John we're all thinking about him and wishing him a fast recovery.

B：That's really kind of you.

- - - - - - - - - - - - - - -

A：瑪麗，聽到妳丈夫出了事故時，我真是嚇壞了！

B：所幸的是已經轉危為安了。

A：如果我能為妳做點什麼，請告訴我。妳去醫院時，我會很樂意照顧孩子們。

B：太感謝了，珍妮，如果不介意的話，我明天可能需要妳的幫忙。

A：一點也不（介意）。請轉告約翰我們都很想他，希望他早日恢復健康。

B：妳真是太好了！

深入分析

★**It's really kind of you.** 你真是太好了！

表達了說話者的感激之情，也可以說 "It's very nice of you." 或是 "You're so nice."，表示中文的「你真是好心腸！」例如：

A：Let me help you with it.

B：Thanks. It's very nice of you.

A：讓我來幫你的忙。

B：謝謝！你真是太好了！

實用・會話・3

A：Cathy, I'm deeply sorry to hear about your grandmother's death. She was such a wonderful person, and we all loved her so much.

B：Thank you for your sympathy, Linda

A：Let me know if there is anything I can do for you.

B：Thanks for the flowers. You are really thoughtful.

A：Well, I'll let you go now. There are a lot of other people waiting to talk to you. I'll see you tomorrow at the funeral service.

B：Thanks again, Linda, for coming.

A：凱西，聽到妳祖母的事，我深感遺憾。她曾 是這麼好的人，而且我們都如此愛她。

B：謝謝妳的同情，琳達。

A：如果我能為妳做什麼，請告訴我。

B：謝謝妳的花，真是太周到了！

A：哦，我不耽擱妳了。許多人在等著和妳說 話。明天葬禮上見吧！

B：琳達，謝謝妳趕過來！

深入分析

You are really thoughtful. 你真是太周到了。

非常適合當成回應對方的慰問，如：

⊙Thank you for your gifts. You are really thoughtful.

謝謝你的禮物。你真是太周到了。

實·用·會·話·4

A：I'm so upset, Jean. I didn't get the promotion.

B：I'm really sorry to hear that. I can't believe this, Bill. You are the best in the office. If anyone deserved it, you did.

A：Thanks for your understanding, Jean. I really did think I was going to get it. That's why it hurts me so much.

B：Don't let it get you down. There'll be other promotions.

A：我很難過，琴。我沒有得到升職。

B：實在是遺憾，我簡直不能相信，比爾。你是這個辦公室最好的，如果有什麼人該升遷的話，那應該是你。

A：感謝妳的理解，琴。我原先真的認為我會升遷的，這就是我感到很受傷的原因。

B：不要因此而氣餒，還會有其他升遷機會的。

深入分析

★get sb. down　使某人感到沮喪

down 除了表示「向下的」之外，也帶有
「情緒低落」的意思，例如：

⊙Don't let the failure get you down.

不要讓這次的失敗使你沮喪。

⊙The bad news got them down.

壞消息使他們很沮喪。

實·用·會·話·5

A：Tom, I'm really sorry to hear that your bike
was stolen. Did you hear anything from the
police?

B：Not yet.

A：Well, if you need to go somewhere, you are
welcome to use mine.

B：Thanks, John. That's very nice of you.

A：湯姆，聽說你的自行車被偷了，我實在為你
難過。警方那兒有什麼消息嗎？

B：還沒有！

A：哦，如果你要去什麼地方，你可以用我的。

B：謝謝，約翰。你真好。

深入分析

★**be welcome to do sth.** 可隨意做某事

welcome 是表示「歡迎」的意思，例如常見的 "Welcome home."（歡迎回家），若是 welcome 後面加 "to+動詞"，則有「允許做某事」的意思，例如：

⊙ You are welcome to use my bike.

你可以用我的自行車。

welcome 還可以有其他的表達：welcome sb. to some place，表示「歡迎某人至某地」，例如：

⊙ Welcome to our school.

歡迎蒞臨我們學校。

Unit 15

贊成和反對

贊成

★ Absolutely!
   絕對正確！

★ Definitely!
   肯定是！

★ You are exactly right!
   你說得太對了！

★ That's exactly right!
   那對極了！

★ I totally agree with what you say!
   我完全同意你所說的。

★ That's exactly what I was thinking!
   那正是我所想的！

★ There's no doubt about it.
   毫無疑問。

★ That's my opinion, too.
   這也是我的意見。

★ Well, I'm not completely sure, but I
   generally agree.
   哦，我沒有十足的把握，但我大致上是同意
   的。

反對

★ You could be right, but don't you think that...?
你可能是對的，但你是否認為…… ？

★ Yes, that's truc, but my feeling is that...
那倒是真的，但我的感覺是……。

★ I understand what you're saying, but in my opinion...
我理解你所説的，但我的意見是……。

★ I hate to disagree with you, but I believe...
我不願和你有分歧，但我相信……。

★ I'm afraid not. I don't see it that way.
恐怕我不是這麼認為的。

★ I don't think so.
我不這麼認為。

★ I don't agree with you.
我不同意你的看法。

★ Are you joking?
你在開玩笑吧 ？

★ I can't believe it.
我不敢相信。

★ You've got to be joking!
　你肯定是在開玩笑！

MP3 102

實·用·會·話·1

A：Tom is a lovely boy.

B：Yes, I quite agree with you.

A：He never tells a lie.

B：Well, yes, that's quite true.

--- --- --- --- --- --- --- --- --- ---

A：湯姆是個可愛的孩子。

B：是的。我很贊成。

A：他從不說謊。

B：噢，是的，的確是。

深·入·分·析

★agree with sb. 同意某人的觀點或意見
　　表示同意某人的觀念，就用 "agree with
sb." 的片語，若是同意某人的某個觀念，
則要加上 "on＋觀念" ，成為 "agree with
sb. on sth." ，例如：
⊙I can't agree with you.
　我不同意你的觀點。
⊙I agree with you on this point.
　這一點我和你的意見一樣。

實·用·會·話·2

A：We're going to New York for summer vacation.

B：Sounds good.

A：Some people say it's a cool place in summer.

B：Well, I think they're right.

- - - - - - - - - - - - - - -

A：我們要去紐約度假了。

B：聽起來不錯呀！

A：有人說那兒的夏天很涼爽。

B：噢，我想他們是對的。

實·用·會·話·3

A：Our neighbor is very noisy.

B：No. I don't think so.

A：Why?

B：Because they're an old couple, and they go to bed very early at night.

- - - - - - - - - - - - - - -

A：我們的鄰居太吵了。

B：不，才不是。

A：為什麼？

B：因為他們是對年老的夫婦，他們晚上都很早睡。

實·用·會·話·4 ●

A：He is really a charming man.

B：Oh, no. I can't agree with you.

A：What do you think of him then?

B：He's got a very bad temper.

- - - - - - - - - - - - - - - -

A：他真是個很有趣的人。

B：才不是！我不認同你的觀點。

A：那你覺得他怎麼樣？

B：他的脾氣很壞！

深入分析

★**have got a bad temper 壞脾氣**

若是好脾氣則是 "a good temper"。

⊙As we all know, his father has got a very
bad temper.

眾所周知，他父親的脾氣不好。

⊙Her mother has got a very good temper.

她媽媽的脾氣很好。

實·用·會·話·5

A : Some say modern dances appeal to young people only.

B : I'm not sure I agree.

A : What makes you think that?

B : If you go to the parks in the morning, you'll see hundreds of elderly people dancing disco.

A : Well, that is a modified form of disco.

B : True. But you also see lots of middle-aged people in disco clubs in the evening.

A : I guess you are right.

━ ━ ━ ━ ━ ━ ━ ━ ━ ━ ━ ━ ━

A：有人說現代舞只有年輕人才喜歡。

B：我不太贊成這個說法。

A：為什麼不贊成？

B：如果你早上去公園，你會看到成百上千的老年人在跳迪斯可。

A：哦，那是一種改良型的迪斯可。

B：說得對。在晚上，在迪斯可俱樂部，你也能看到許多中年人。

A：我想你是對的。

深入分析

★**What makes you think that?** 你為什麼會
這麼認為？

當對方提出的觀念你感到質疑時，就可以說
「你為什麼會這麼認為？」英文就叫做
"What makes you think that?" 字面意思是
「是什麼原因造成你的想法」，相同意思也
可以說 "What makes you think so?"，注
意的是，make 要用單數動詞 makes 表示。

實·用·會·話·6

A : My teacher told me that students should learn to think independently. Do you agree?

B : Definitely! Unfortunately, I don't think many teachers are teaching their students that way.

A : You are absolutely right.

B : You know what they should do? They should give us more opportunities to express our opinions and not be too strict about what is correct or wrong.

A : That's a good idea.

A：我的老師告訴我說學生應該學會獨立思考。你贊成嗎？

B：絕對贊成！不幸的是，我認為許多老師並不都是那樣來教導學生的。

A：你說的對極了！

B：你知道他們該怎麼辦嗎？他們應給我們更多的機會來表達我們的觀點，而且在對與錯的問題上不要太嚴格。

A：這是個好主意！

深入分析

1. absolutely 完全地、絕對地

雖然是副詞，但在口語英文中，也可單獨使用，表示「正確」、「當然」的意思，相同意思也可以用 definitely 表示，例如：

A：So you decided to go with her?

B：Absolutely.

A：所以你已經決定和她一起去？

B：沒錯！

A：Are you going to David's birthday party?

B：Definitely

A：你有要去大衛的生日派對嗎？

B：那是一定的。

2. Unfortunately, ... 不幸地，…

fortunate 是「幸運的」形容詞，否定用法則在字首加 un，成為 unfortunate，兩者分別衍生出「幸運地」及「不幸地」的副詞用法：

⊙Unfortunately, he's dead.

不幸的是，他死了。

⊙Fortunately, we survived.

幸運的是，我們存活下來了！

實·用·會·話·7

A：By the way, how do you like the music they are playing?

B：It's pop music. Pop music isn't bad; but personally I prefer classical music.

A：Some say pop music is not pleasant to hear. Don't you think so?

B：I wouldn't say it's unpleasant. Pop music is exciting and stimulating.

A：But why do you like classical music more?

B：Well, it is only a matter of taste. Maybe I am a more conservative type of person.

— — — — — — — — — — — — —

A：你覺得他們演奏的音樂怎麼樣？

B：是流行樂。流行樂不錯，但我個人更喜歡古典音樂。

A：有人說流行音樂聽起來不舒服。你不這樣認為嗎？

B：我不會說不舒服。流行樂很能振奮人心。

A：那你為什麼更喜歡古典音樂？

B：哦，這只是個人品味的問題。或許我是更保守類型的人吧！

實·用·會·話·8

A：Some people say owning a private car is too expensive. What's your opinion of it?

B：I'm not sure I can agree. I'd say cars are very important means of transportation.

A：You still didn't convince me.

B：Well, only time will tell. You will see more and more people driving their own cars.

A：But what about the streets and traffic jams?

B：Well, that's a different issue. You can't tell people not to buy cars simply because the streets are not wide enough, can you?

A：有人說擁有私人汽車是太過於昂貴的。你有什麼觀點？

B：我不這麼同意。我認為汽車是一種非常重要的交通工具。

A：你還沒有說服我。

B：噢，時間會證明一切。你會看到越來越多的人駕駛著他們自己的汽車。

A：但是街道和交通擁塞怎麼辦呢？

B：哦，這倒是個難解的問題。你不能單單因為街道不夠寬而叫人們不要買車，是吧？

A : Hello, Jim. I heard you have a new secretary.

B : Yeah, for only two weeks. Her name is Mary.

A : What do you think of her?

B : So far she has been doing OK.

A : Just OK?

B : Well, to be fair, more than OK. It's though still too early to tell. She is very familiar with office routine, such as typing, filing, and taking phone calls.

A : How about her as a person, say, her manner and personality?

B : Oh, she is a very pleasant lady. She speaks softly and politely. She is very patient with our clients and very helpful with colleagues.

A : How do you like her dress and makeup?

B : Wait a second. Why do you want to know so many details about her?

A : Well, to tell you the truth, Mary is my younger sister.

A：喂，吉姆，聽說你有了個新秘書。

B：是啊，有兩個星期了。她叫瑪麗。

A：你認為她怎麼樣？

B：到目前她表現得還不錯。

A：只是還不錯？

B：哦，坦白地說，比還不錯要好些，儘管現在下結論還太早。她非常熟悉辦公室的工作，例如打字、整理歸檔、接電話。

A：她為人如何？例如舉止和個性？

B：噢，她是個非常爽快的人。說話輕柔有禮，耐心對待客戶，也常常幫忙同事。

A：她的服飾和打扮怎麼樣？

B：等一下，為什麼你想瞭解這麼多關於她的事？

A：哦，告訴你實話吧，瑪麗是我妹妹。

107

1. be familiar with...　對……很熟悉

可以表示對某事物或人物很瞭解、熟悉或認識的意思，例如：

A：Are you familiar with Miss Green?

B：Yes, I am.

A：你對格林小姐很熟悉嗎？

B：對，是很熟啊！

2. so far　到目前為止

用於完成時態中，表示至目前為止的狀態說明，例如：

⊙So far they haven't heard of it.

　　到目前為止，他們還沒有聽說此事。

另一種常見的 "so far" 慣用語則是在問候的情境中："so far so good"，表示「目前為止一切都很好」的意思，例如：

A：How are you doing?

B：So far so good. And you?

A：你好嗎？

B：目前為止都還不錯！你呢？

拜訪

★ Will it be all right to visit you tonight?
今晚我可以去拜訪你嗎？

★ Do you mind if I call on you this evening?
你介意我今晚去拜訪你嗎？

★ I'd be happy if you come.
你能來我會很高興。

★ I'll be expecting you at home.
我會在家等你。

★ It's very nice of you to come.
你能來真是太好了。

★ How about some coffee?
來點咖啡如何？

★ Would you like something to drink?
你想喝點什麼嗎？

★ What would you like to drink, tea or coffee?
你想喝什麼，茶還是咖啡？

★ Please don't bother.
別麻煩了！

★ Coffee, please.
我喝咖啡就好，謝謝！

★ Make yourself at home.
請自便。

實·用·會·話·1

A：Oh, it's you. I've been expecting you.

B：Glad to see you. May I come in?

A：Please. I miss you so much.

B：Same with me. So I must come here.

A：Tea or coffee?

B：Tea, please. How are things going recently?

A：Just fine. How about you?

B：Just so-so. David told me that you'll direct a new film.

A：That's right.

B：That's great! I'm sure you'll make a great success.

— — — — — — — — — — — — —

A：噢，是你。我一直在等你。

B：真高興見到你。我能進來嗎？

A：快請進！我真的很想念你啊！

B：我也是。所以我一定得來。

A：喝茶還是咖啡？

B：請來點茶。最近怎麼樣？

A：還好。你呢？

B：馬馬虎虎。大衛告訴我說你將導演一部新片子。是真的嗎？

A：沒錯！

B：太棒了！我確定你一定成功的。

深入分析

🎧 109

★**How things go recently?** 近來如何？

通常是朋友之間的寒暄之詞，以表示關心的問候，例如你可以說 "I haven't seen you for several days. How things go recently?"，表示「好幾天沒見你了。近來如何？」，相同意思也可以有類似的用法，"How are things going recently?"

A：How things go recently?

B：Not too bad.

A：近來進展如何？

B：還不錯！

A : Excuse me, Prof. Smith. I have some questions to discuss with you. I wonder if it will be all right to visit you in the afternoon.

B : I'd be happy if you could come, but this afternoon is all booked up. What about tomorrow afternoon?

A : Well, I have classes tomorrow afternoon.

B : Maybe you can come to my house this evening.

A : What time will it be all right?

B : How about 8 o'clock after I have my dinner?

A : That's fine.

B : All right then. I'll be expecting you.

(In the evening)

A : Is Prof. Smith in?

B : Hi, come on in. Make yourself at home. What would you like to drink, coffee or tea?

A : Tea, please.

A：對不起，史密斯教授。我有幾個問題想和你討
論一下。不知道今天下午拜訪你是否合適。

B：你能來我很高興，但今天下午(我的)行程排
滿了。明天下午怎麼樣？

A：哦，明天下午我有課。

B：或許今天晚上你可以到我家來。

A：幾點鐘方便呢？

B：我吃過晚飯後，八點鐘怎麼樣？

A：好的！

B：那好，我等你！

（晚上）

A：史密斯教授在嗎？

B：嗨！進來吧。請不要拘束啊！你想喝什麼，
咖啡還是茶？

A：我喝茶，謝謝！

110

1. be booked up 時間已排滿

若是指位子已經客滿或是時間排滿,都可以說 "be booked up" ,例如:

⊙This week is booked up.

這週時間已排滿了。

⊙The theater is booked up.

劇院 (座位) 已坐滿了。

2. make sb. at home 不要拘束

當你要招待訪客,都希望對方要像在自己家裡一樣自在,中文是「不要拘束」,英文則是 "make yourself at home" ,例如:

⊙Please make yourself at home.

請不要拘束。

⊙What he said made mc at home.

他的話使我很自在。

實·用·會·話·3

A : What happened, happened. Let it go.

B : It's not easy for me.

A : I know. Well, it's getting late. I'm afraid I must be leaving now.

B : Just stay a little bit longer.

A : I'd like to but I have to be going. I had a good time today. Thank you for everything.

B : You're welcome. Good night.

A : Good night.

A : 覆水難收。看開一點吧！

B : 對我來說是很難熬！

A : 我瞭解！這樣吧，不早了。我想我得走了。

B : 再多待一會兒吧！

A : 我很想啊，可是我必須走了。今天過得很愉快。謝謝你所做的一切。

B : 別客氣！晚安！

A : 晚安！

111

深入分析

**1. What happened, happened.
已經發生的事，就發生了！**

中文常說的「覆水難收」就是 "What happened, happened."，類似安慰對方既然已經發生了，就不要再鑽牛角尖想不開了，該是接受這個事實的時候了！例如：

A：I don't really know how to face her family.

B：What happened, happened.

A：我真不知道該如何面對她的家人。

B：已經發生的事，就發生了！

2. I'd like to...　我想要……

是 "I would like to…" 的縮寫，是一種禮貌性的客氣用語，表示「我想要……」的意思，例如：

A：Would you like to go to a movie with me?

B：I'd like to, but I can't.

A：你今晚想和我一起去看電影嗎？

B：我很想去，但是我不能去。

16
拜訪

實·用·會·話·4

A : I'm very sorry, but I won't be able to come over to your new house tomorrow morning. I have to meet a friend at the airport.

B : That's all right. We can make it some other time. Suppose we can meet next Sunday.

A : Fine. I'll call you then.

B : OK. Bye.

A：很抱歉，明天早上我不能到你的新房子來了。我得去機場接一位朋友。

B：沒關係、我們可以另約時間。下個星期天怎麼樣。

A：好的。到時我打電話給你。

B：好吧。再見！

★meet sb. at the airport
去機場接某人的飛機
中文常說的「接送」,在英文用法中,則沒有任何「接送」的字眼,只要用 meet(見面)的動詞即可,例如:
A：Is someone meeting you here?
B：Yeah, my husband.
A：有人來接你嗎?
B：有,我先生。

🎵 112

實·用·會·話·5

A：Good morning, Mr. Brown.
B：Oh, David. Come on in.
A：Thanks. Nice day, isn't it?
B：Yes, a nice day. Let me get you something to drink, coffee or tea?
A：Just water, please. I wonder if you could tell me how to improve my oral English.
B：If you want to improve it in a short time, there is only one way, that's you must speak English at any time you can.
A：Yes, I know. But in what way?

B：For example, you can speak English in class and talk with your classmates or discuss something with your teacher.

A：I see.

B：You can also listen to the radio or watch TV.

A：Of course.

B：I'm sure you can speak English very well someday.

A：I hope so. I'm sorry, but I must go now. Thank you for your time.

B：No problem. Goodbye.

— — — — — — — — — — — — — — — — —

A：早安，伯朗先生。

B：噢，是大衛啊。進來吧！

A：多謝啦！天氣不錯，是吧？

B：是啊，一個好天氣。我給你弄點喝的，茶還是咖啡？

A：喝水就好。你能否給我建議怎樣提高我的英語口語能力。

B：如果你想在短期內提高口語表達能力，只有一個可行的辦法，那就是利用一切機會說英語。

A：是的，我知道了。但怎麼去說呢？

B：例如，你可以在班上說英語，和你的同學講話或和老師討論問題時也說英語。

A：我知道了。

B：你還可以聽收音機或看電視。

A：沒問題！

B：我相信有一天，你的英語能說得很好。

A：我也希望如此。很抱歉，我該走了。感謝你的時間。

B：不客氣！

16
拜訪

深入分析

★for example　舉例來說

這是一句非常實用的口語化英文,當要解釋觀念或見解時,需要有例子佐證,此時就適合在句首說 "for example,..."。類似的用法也可以說 "for instance"。

A：What shall I do?

B：For example, go see a doctor. Maybe it will help.

A：我該怎麼辦?

B：例如去看醫生吧!也許會有幫助。

實·用·會·話·6

A：Good morning, Mr. Brown. May I come in?

B：Certainly you can. Come in, please.

A：Not a bad day!

B：Yes. What would you like to drink'?

A：Tea, please. I often heard Peter mention you when I was in Taiwan. He asked me to visit you when I came to America.

B：Thanks. How are things going with Peter?

A：Very good. He is studying in Taiwan University and misses you very much. How about you recently?

B：Not bad, I have a book published recently.

A：Congratulations! You are always good.

B：Thank you.

A：It's too late now. I think I should go now. See you.

B：Goodbye.

16
拜
訪

- - - - - - - - - - - - - -

A：早安， 布朗先生。 我可以進來嗎？

B：當然可以。請進！

A：今天天氣不錯！

B：是啊。喝點什麼？

A：我喝茶。我在台灣時常聽彼得談起你，我來美國的時候他請我來看看你。

B：謝謝。彼得過得怎麼樣？

A：很好。他在台灣大學讀書，時常想念你。你最近過得好嗎？

B：還不錯，最近出了一本書。

A：恭喜你！你一直都很棒。

B：謝謝！

A：時間不早了。我該走了。再見！

B：再見！

深入分析

★**How are things going?** 事情進展如何？

問候對方除了可以說 "How do you do?" 之外，也可以針對「事情的進展」問候對方，例如：

A：How are things going?

B：Not too bad.

A：一切進展如何？

B：還不錯。

邀 請

提出邀請

★ How about having dinner with me tonight?
要不要今晚和我一起吃飯？

★ How would you like to go to a movie tonight?
你今天晚上要去看電影嗎？

★ Would you like to see the new film?
你想去看這部新電影嗎？

★ Are you going to be busy this evening?
今晚忙嗎？

★ Do you have any plans next Sunday?
你下個星期天有任何計劃嗎？

★ I was wondering if you would like to go to the movie with me.
不知道你是不是想和我去看電影。

★ I wonder if you would be free this afternoon.
不知道你今天下午是否有空。

★ Lets' go swimming.
我們去游泳吧！

★ Why don't we go dancing?
要不要去跳舞！

邀請的時間

★ What time would be convenient for you?
什麼時間對你合適？

★ Would Tuesday morning suit you?
星期二早晨對你合適嗎？

★ What about Friday afternoon?
星期五下午怎麼樣？

★ How would 10:30?
十點半如何？

★ Would 7:00 be OK?
七點鐘可以嗎？

★ Let's say about 6:00.
我們約六點點鐘！

★ I'll pick you up around 10:30.
我大概會在十點半來接你！

回應對方的邀請

★ I'd love to.
我願意。

★ That's a great idea.
好主意。

★ That sounds great.
聽起來不錯。

★ I'll be free tomorrow afternoon.
明天下午我有空。

★ Thanks for asking, but I don't think so.
謝謝邀請，我不能答應。

★ I'm sorry, but Tuesday won't be so convenient for me.
對不起，但星期二我不太方便。

★ I'm afraid I can't make it today.
今天恐怕不行。

★ I'm afraid tonight is a bit of problem.
恐怕今晚有點問題。

★ I'd rather stay home and watch TV.
我寧願待在家裡看電視。

實·用·會·話·1

A：Are you free this evening, Jim?

B：Yes. Why?

A：Do you feel like going to the new mall?

B：Oh, that's a good idea.

A：Good. What's the best time to meet?

B：Let's say about 8:00?

A：That's OK with me.

- - - - - - - - - - - - - - - - -

A：今晚有空嗎，吉姆？

B：有啊。怎麼了？

A：你想去那一家新開張的商場嗎？

B：噢，好主意。

A：太好了！什麼時候見面比較好？

B：我們就約大約八點鐘好嗎？

A：我可以！

17 邀請

深入分析

★feel like... 想要…

後面通常接名詞或動名詞子句，表示「願意去做…」的意思，例如：

⊙Do you feel like having a cup of coffee?

你想喝杯咖啡嗎？

⊙We'll go for a walk, if you feel like it.

如果你願意，我們去散散步。

MP3 116

實·用·會·話·2

A：Jim, are you doing anything special this weekend?

B：Yes. Peter and I have promised to call on a new customer.

A：Oh, well, never mind. But I was thinking of asking you and your wife to go out for dinner.

B：That sounds great. I wonder if we could make it some other time.

A：How about Sunday evening, at 7 o'clock?

B：That'll be all right. See you then.

A：吉姆，這個週末有什麼事嗎？

B：有啊！彼得和我答應過去拜訪一位新顧客。

A：哦，那沒關係。我是想邀請你和你太太出來吃飯。

B：那好啊！要不要另外約個時間？

A：星期天晚上，七點鐘？

B：好，到時候見。

深入分析

17
邀請

★call on 拜訪

"call on" 和「打電話」完全沒有關係，而是指「拜訪某人」的意思，常用句型為 "call on sb." ，例如：

⊙Tomorrow we'll call on Prof. Smith.

明天我們將拜訪史密斯教授。

⊙When are you going to call on your teacher?

你打算何時拜訪你的老師？

實·用·會·話·3

(On the phone)

A：Dr. Anderson's office. May I help you?

B：Yes. I'd like to make an appointment for a physical checkup.

A：Are you a regular patient?

B：No, I'm not. I recently moved to this area.

A：I see. I'm afraid Dr. Anderson can't see you this week. Will next Monday morning be all right?

B：OK. What time would you like me to come? Suppose I come at 8:00?

A：Good. We'll see you then.

（電話中）

A：安德森醫生辦公室。需要我效勞嗎？

B：我想約個時間做體檢。

A：你是定期的病人嗎？

B：不是。我最近剛搬到這個地區。

A：我明白了。恐怕這週安德森醫生不能見你。下週一早上可以嗎？

B：好的。我要幾點來呢？八點鐘可以嗎？

A：好，就八點鐘吧！

★make an appointment 預約

make an appointment 通常是指「預約」，
例如：

A：I'd like to make an appointment with Dr.
　　Jones. Would 9:00 be all right?

B：I'm afraid not. He doesn't have any
　　openings in the morning.

A：我要和瓊斯醫師約時間。明天九點鐘可
　　以嗎？

B：恐怕不行！他當天早上沒有名額了！

appointment 通常是正式的會面，而非情侶
間的「約會」（date）例如：

⊙I have an appointment with my dentist at
　3 pm.

　我已約定下午三點鐘去看牙醫。

⊙I'll have a date tonight.

　今晚我有約會。

實·用·會·話·4

A：Oh, Mr. Brown, I'm sorry, I won't be able to keep my appointment with you for Thursday. You see, I have to fly to Hong Kong this afternoon on urgent business. Could we postpone our meeting to sometime early next week?

B：Certainly. What about Monday morning?

A：That would be fine. Shall we make it 9 o'clock?

B：All right.

A：I'm very sorry about Thursday.

B：Oh, that's quite all right. I understand perfectly.

- - - - - - - - - - - - - - - -

A：哦，伯朗先生，對不起，星期四我不能赴約了。我今天下午因有急事得飛往香港。我們能把會面延到下週早些時候嗎？

B：當然可以。星期一早上怎麼樣？

A：好的，那我們就約在九點鐘好嗎？

B：好啊！

A：星期四的事我很抱歉！

B：哦，沒關係，我能理解。

118

深入分析

★keep one's appointment　實踐約定

字面意思是「保留約定」，也就是「遵守諾言」的意思，例如：

⊙I think you should keep your appointment.

我想你應該遵守諾言。

⊙Today I'm so tired. Maybe I won't be able to keep my appointment.

今天我太累了，也許我得失約了。

17
邀
請

實·用·會·話·5

A：When can we expect you for dinner? Can you come tonight?

B：Not tonight. I promised to go to a concert with Joe.

A：Well, how about Friday then?

B：That sounds fine.

A：Good. Shall we say 7 o'clock?

B：Sure. I'll be there.

- - - - - - - - - - - - - - - - - -

A：什麼時候我們能一起吃晚飯？今晚你能來嗎？

B：今晚不行。我答應和喬伊一起去參加音樂會。

A：那麼，星期五行嗎？

B：聽起來是可以的！

A：太好了！我們約在七點鐘好嗎？

B：好，我會過去的。

★**how about...　你認為……怎麼樣？**

表示提出建議希望得到對方評論的意思，在 "how about" 後面可以接名詞或動名詞式子句，例如：

⊙How about this pair of shoes?

　這雙鞋子怎麼樣？

⊙How about having a dinner with me?

　和我吃晚餐如何？

MP3 119

實·用·會·話·6

(On the phone)

A：Hello! May I speak to Mr. Smith, please?

B：This is John Smith speaking.

A：Good morning, Mr. Smith. This is Mary speaking. I'm very sorry to say I have to put off our appointment for this afternoon from three to five, because something urgent has just come up.

B：I'm afraid I have another appointment at five. How about tomorrow afternoon? Would that be too late?

A：No. That'll be all right. When will it be convenient for you?

B：How about two o'clock?

A：All right. I'm sorry about this change. See you tomorrow.

B：See you then.

（電話中）

A：喂！我可以與史密斯先生通話嗎？

B：我就是約翰・史密斯。

A：早安，史密斯先生。我是瑪麗。很抱歉，因為有急事，我得將我們今天下午的約會從三點延到五點鐘。

B：我五點鐘另外有約。明天下午怎麼樣？那樣會太晚嗎？

A：可以，不晚。你幾點鐘方便？

B：兩點鐘怎麼樣？

A：好啊！我很抱歉要改時間。明天見！

B：到時見！

深入分析

★come up 出現、發生

就字面意思來說 "come up" 代表「出現」
的意思，另一層意思則有「發生某事」的解
釋。

⊙A stranger suddenly came up.

突然一個陌生人出現了。

⊙I don't know when it came up.

我不知道那是何時發生的。

17 邀請

看醫生

詢問症狀

★ What's wrong with your leg?
你的腿怎麼了？

★ What's the matter with you?
你怎麼了？

★ What seems to be the trouble?
怎麼回事？

★ Aren't you feeling well?
你感覺不舒服嗎？

★ How long have you been like this?
你像這樣有多長的時間了？

★ How long have you had it?
這樣的症狀有多長的時間了？

★ How long has this been going on?
像這樣有多長的時間了？

★ Since when have you felt like this?
從什麼時候起有這種感覺的？

★ How long has it hurt?
痛多久了？

★ Can you bend over and touch your toes?
你可以彎腰摸到你的腳指嗎？

★ When did it happen?
什麼時候發生的？

★ Let's have a look.
我看看！

★ Let me take a look at it.
我看一下！

★ Let me check your blood pressure.
讓我量量你的血壓。

★ I think I'd better take an X-ray.
我覺得最好照X光。

 121

18
看醫生

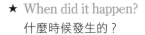

患者說明症狀

★ I don't feel well.
我感覺不好。

★ I really feel awful.
我覺得很糟糕。

★ I've got a high fever and I feel dizzy.
我發高燒而且頭很暈。

★ I seem to be çatching a cold.
我好像感冒了。

★ I woke up with a terrible headache and I have a fever.
我起床後頭很痛，而且我發燒了。

★ My throat hurts, too.
我的喉嚨也很痛。

★ My shoulder hurts.
我的肩膀會痛。

★ But my back still hurts.
可是我的背還是很痛。

★ I cut my finger on Sunday, but the cut wasn't too bad.
我星期天切到手，但是不嚴重。

★ Should I change my diet?
我需要改變飲食嗎？

診斷結果

★ Nothing serious.
沒什麼嚴重。

★ It's just a cold. There is nothing to worry about.
只是感冒，沒什麼好擔心的。

★ I think you've got the flu.
我覺得你得到流感了！

★ It sounds as if you have a virus.
聽起來你感染病毒了！

★ It's probably a virus.
可能是病毒。

★ It feels as if you've got a fever.
你應該是發燒了！

★ You'll need treatment.
你需要接受治療。

★ You have to stop smoking.
你得戒菸。

★ You have to stop drinking.
你得戒酒。

★ Try to eat less fat and salt.
試著少吃脂肪和鹽巴。

★ You should lose some weight.　　**MP3** 122
你應該要減肥。

★ You should stay in bed for a few days.
你應該臥床幾天。

★ Have a good rest.
好好休息。

★ You should get some rest.
　你應該要多休息。

★ You'd better stay in bed for a couple of days.
　你最好臥床休息一兩天。

★ I want you to take it easy.
　你要放輕鬆點。

★ Take a few days off from work and don't
　wear yourself out.
　放假幾天，不要太勞累！

★ You can take aspirin for your headache.
　頭痛可以吃阿司匹靈。

實·用·會·話·1

A：What's the trouble?

B：I've got a sore throat and my chest hurts,
　　and I feel a bit dizzy.

A：How long have you been like this?

B：Two or three days.

A：Do you have a headache?

B：Yes, I do. And I think I've got a fever, too.

A：Do you sneeze?

B：Yes.

A：Let me take your temperature and listen to
　　your lungs. Well, I think you've caught the flu.

B：What do you advise, doctor?

A：Take this prescription to the drugstore for the medicine.

B：How should I take the medicine?

A：Take one big tablet and two small ones three times a day after meals. Furthermore, there is nothing better for you than plenty of water and sleep.

- - - - - - - - - - - - - - - - -

A：怎麼了？

B：我喉嚨疼，胸部也疼，感覺有點頭暈。

A：有多久的時間了？

B：兩三天了。

A：頭疼嗎？

B：有。我也有發燒。

A：打噴嚏嗎？

B：有。

A：我給你量量體溫，聽聽你的肺部。哦，我想你是得了流感。

B：你有什麼建議，醫生？

A：把這個藥方拿到藥房去取藥。

B：藥怎麼服用呢？

A：大的一片，小的兩片，一日三次，飯後服用。還有，你最好多多喝水，充足睡眠。

深入分析

1. What's the trouble with you? 你怎麼了？

What's the matter with...?意思是「……怎麼了？」是醫生看診時一種非常實用句型，例如：

A：What's the trouble with you?

B：I have got a cold.

A：你怎麼了？

B：我感冒了。

2. take one's temperature 給某人量體溫

⊙The doctor is going to take his temperature.

醫生將給他量體溫。

⊙Have you taken your son's temperature?

你給你兒子量過體溫了嗎？

3. My chest hurts. 我胸痛。

常見的疼痛說明語句有以下幾種：

⊙My arm hurts.

我的手臂會痛。

⊙My leg hurts.

我的腿會痛。

⊙My foot hurts.

我的腳會痛。

實·用·會·話·2

A：What is the matter with you?

B：I have a terrible toothache.

A：Which tooth is it?

B：This one here. How bad is it?

A：There's a big cavity.

B：Can you fill it?

A：I'm afraid not. It's too late. It'll have to be taken out.

B：Then I want to have it taken out now.

A：You'd better wait. The gums are swollen. Take the medicine I give and come back in three days.

18 看醫生

— — — — — — — — — — — — — — — —

A：哪裡不舒服？

B：我的牙疼得厲害。

A：哪一顆牙？

B：這邊的這顆。有多糟？

A：啊，是的。有一個大洞。

B：你能把它補上嗎？

A：恐怕不能，太遲了。必須把它拔掉。

B：那我想現在就拔掉。

A：你最好等一等。牙床有點腫。服用我給你開的藥，三天後再來。

實·用·會·話·3

A：What's the matter with you?

B：I slipped on the icy road and fell down.

A：Are you hurt?

B：I think my arm is broken.

A：Oh! Which arm is it?

B：The right one. It hurts right here.

A：Let me see.

B：What do you think?

A：You'd better have an X-ray.

B：Is it serious?

A：I'm not sure. Wait until we get the report from the lab.

- - - - - - - - - - - - - - - -

A：你怎麼了？

B：我在結冰的路上滑了一下，摔倒了。

A：受傷了嗎？

B：我想我的手臂斷了。

A：噢，哪一隻手臂？

B：右臂。就這兒疼。

A：我瞧瞧。

B：你覺得怎麼樣了？

A：你最好拍一張 X 光片。

B：嚴重嗎？

A：我不敢肯定。等攝影室的報告出來再說吧！

深入分析　　　　　　　　　🎧 125

> ★**had better do...** 最好做……
>
> 可縮寫為 "sb.'d better do..."，是建議某人
> 做某事之意如：
>
> ⊙ You'd better have a rest.
> 　你最好休息一下。
>
> ⊙ You'd better give up the foolish idea.
> 　你最好放棄這愚蠢的想法。

⑱ 看醫生

A：Is it serious, doctor?

B：No, just a bad cold.

A：I hope it won't last long.

B：It shouldn't if you take good care of yourself.

A：What do you think I ought to do?

B：Take the medicine I've prescribed and get plenty of rest.

A：Do I have to go on a diet?

B：It's not necessary. Drink plenty of water and since your stomach is upset, avoid eating too much oily food.

- - - - - - - - - - - - - -

A：嚴重嗎，醫生？

B：不嚴重，只是重感冒。

A：我希望不會持續太長時間。

B：好好照顧自己，病情就不會持續太久。

A：你覺得我應該怎麼做？

B：服用我給你開的藥，多多休息。

A：我要控制飲食嗎？

B：不必要。多喝水，既然你胃不舒服，就避免
吃太多油膩的食物。

 深 入 分 析　　　　　MP3 126

★**go on a diet**　吃規定的飲食（節食）

也可以用 "be on a diet" 表示「正在節食」
或「正在控制飲食」的意思，例如：

⊙The doctor asked me to go on a diet, for I
was too fat.

醫生讓我吃規定的飲食，因為我太胖了。

⊙I think the fat should go on a diet.

我認為肥胖的人應該節食。

⊙I'm on a diet now.

我現在正在節食中。

實·用·會·話·5

A：Doctor, whenever I cough I have a burning sensation in my throat and my chest hurts.

B：Are you coughing up phlegm?

A：Yes, and it smells terrible.

B：I hear a wheezing sound. Do you have difficulty breathing?

A：Yes, I do.

B：How long have you been feeling this way?

A：About a week.

━ ━ ━ ━ ━ ━ ━ ━ ━ ━ ━

A：醫生，每當我咳嗽時，（喉嚨）就有灼痛的感覺，而且胸部也會痛。

B：你有沒有咳出痰來？

A：有，而且很難聞。

B：我聽到哮喘的聲音。你有沒有呼吸困難的現象？

A：有。

B：這樣狀況有多久了？

A：大約一個星期了。

⑱ 看醫生

深入分析

★**have difficulty (in) doing sth.**

做某事有困難

表示「做某事使很困難的」，通常在 in 的
後面會加動名詞說明，例如：

⊙ Do you think you still have any difficulty
   in spelling?

   你認為你在拼字方面還有困難嗎？

⊙ I have difficulty in speaking English
   fluently.

   我無法說流利的英語。

⊙ I have no difficulty working out this
   problem.

   我毫不費力地算出這道題。

實·用·會·話·6

A : I feel quite sick, doctor.

B : What symptoms do you have?

A : I have a runny nose and can't stop coughing.

B : Do you have a fever?

A : I took my temperature just before I left home, and it was 38.5℃.

B : Have you been vomiting?

A : No, I haven't.

B : Well, you should rest for two or three days. I'll prescribe some medicine.

A : Thank you.

18 看醫生

- - - - - - - - - - - - - - - -

A：我病得很重，醫生。

B：你有什麼症狀？

A：我流鼻涕而且不停地咳嗽。

B：有沒有發燒？

A：我離家之前量過體溫，攝氏三十八度半。

B：有沒有嘔吐？

A：沒有！

B：噢，你應該休息兩天，我會開些藥給你。

A：謝謝！

深入分析

1. prescribe 開（藥方）

通常醫生會針對病人的狀況給予用藥的治療，也就是「開藥方」，就會使用 prescribe 這個單字，例如：

⊙ The doctor has prescribed some medicines for the little girl.

醫生已為小女孩開了一些藥。

⊙ What do you prescribe for this illness?

你對此病開什麼藥方？

而 prescribe 除了是「開藥方」之外，也可以是「提出建議」的意思，例如：

⊙ My doctor prescribed rest and gave me a painkiller for my knee.

我的醫生要我多休息，還給我的膝蓋開了止痛藥。

2. a runny nose 流鼻水

可別誤會為「會跑動的鼻子」，而是暗喻「鼻子流鼻水」，例如：

⊙ I have a runny nose.

我流鼻水了！

稱讚他人

稱讚

★ You are looking fine.
你看起來氣色很好！

★ You look smart.
你看起來很棒！

★ You look beautiful.
你看起來美麗！

★ You look handsome.
你看起來瀟灑！

★ You don't look your age.
你看起來比實際年齡還年輕！

★ You've lost some weight.
你瘦了！

★ This is great.
很好！

★ Good.
很好！

★ Good job.
幹得好！

★ You've done a good job.
做得不錯！

- ★ How nice!
  太好了！

- ★ Wonderful!
  妙極了！

- ★ What a beautiful sweater!
  好漂亮的毛線衫！

- ★ What a pretty necklace!
  好美的項鍊！

- ★ Your tie looks good on you.
  你的領帶很適合你！

- ★ That dress looks great on you.
  你穿那衣服看起來很棒！

- ★ You look great in that new dress.
  你穿那新衣服看起來很棒！

- ★ Your blouse goes beautifully with that skirt.
  你的襯衫配那裙子很好看！

- ★ Your belt goes just right with your blue pants.
  你的腰帶正好配那條藍色褲子！

- ★ It looks smart.
  看起來很棒！

★ It looks terrific.
  看起來很棒！

★ That's absolutely super.　　　**MP3** 129
  那絕對是出色！

★ That's a smart car.
  那是輛很棒的車！

★ I like your new coat.
  我喜歡你的新外套。

回應對方的讚美

★ Thank you. It's very nice of you to say so.
  謝謝你！你能這麼說真是好！

★ Thank you very much for saying so.
  非常感謝你這麼說！

★ I'm flattered.
  我真是受寵若驚！

★ You flatter me.
  你恭維我！

★ I'm glad you like it.
  我很高興你喜歡！

★ Thank you. And yours is nice, too.
謝謝！你的也很不錯！

★ Thank you for the compliment.
多謝讚美！

 130

實·用·會·話·1

A：How do you like this tie?

B：It looks good on you.

A：What about the color?

B：It's nice.

A：Isn't it too bright?

B：No, it's perfect. It goes well with that suit.

— — — — — — — — — — — — —

A：你覺得這條領帶怎麼樣？

B：這條領帶看起來不錯啊！

A：顏色呢？

B：不錯呀！

A：不會太亮嗎？

B：不，很完美。和那件西裝配起來很好。

19 稱讚他人

深入分析

★go well with... 和……搭配得很好

不是「一起去」的意思，"go well with"
在此處是「和……搭配得很好」的意思，例
如：

⊙I like this tie because it goes well with my
suit.

我喜歡這條領帶，因為它和我的套裝搭配
得很好。

⊙They don't think the pair of shoes goes
well with my dress.

他們認為這雙鞋子和我的衣服搭配得不
好。

實·用·會·話·2

A：That's a marvelous jacket.

B：Does it really look OK?

A：Yes, and I like the color and design, too. It
matches your pants well.

B：I got it on sale when I was in Taipei last
month.

A：You were lucky to get it.

A：那件上衣很不錯喔！

B：看起來真的不錯嗎？

A：是的，而且我也喜歡這顏色和款式。和你的褲子很相配！

B：這是我上個月在台北大減價時買的。

A：你可真走運（買到這件）。

★**It matches your pants.** 和你的褲子很相配。

"match" 除了有「比賽」、「較量」的意思外，還表示「相當」、「相配」，表示兩者之間的協調性相當高，例如：

⊙ The carpets should match the curtains.
地毯應該和窗簾相配。

⊙ She was wearing a brown dress with hat and gloves to match.
她穿著一件棕色的衣服，並有帽子和手套相配。

實·用·會·話·3 ●┄┄┄┄┄┄┄┄┄┄●

A：Hi, Tracy. You look great tonight!

B：Thank you. By the way, you look terrific with your new tie.

A：Really? Thanks. Your dress is really beautiful.

B：It's a present from my boy friend.

━ ━ ━ ━ ━ ━ ━ ━ ━ ━ ━ ━

A：嗨，崔西。妳今晚看起來真漂亮！

B：謝謝。對了，你繫的新領帶看起來很棒。

A：是嗎？謝謝。妳的衣服真漂亮！

B：是我男友給我的禮物。

實·用·會·話·4 ●┄┄┄┄┄┄┄┄┄┄●

A：I like your shirt.

B：Do you really like it?

A：Yes, it fits perfectly.

B：It's pure silk, but it wasn't very expensive.

A：That's amazing. It certainly looks expensive.

━ ━ ━ ━ ━ ━ ━ ━ ━ ━ ━ ━

A：我喜歡你的襯衫。

B：你真的喜歡嗎？

A：真的。非常合身。

B：是純絲的，但並不是太貴。

A：太不可思議了！看起來很名貴的呀！

實·用·會·話·5

A：Cathy, you really can sing, can't you?

B：I used to be a member of the school choir.

A：No wonder you can control your voice so well. You are a professional singer.

B：Well, I wouldn't say I am a professional, but I did receive some training at school. My music teacher used to be a professional singer.

A：Well, a good teacher makes good students.

B：You got this one right.

= = = = = = = = = = = = = =

A：凱西，妳唱得真不賴，不是嗎？

B：我過去是學校樂團的成員。

A：怪不得妳的嗓音控制得這麼好，原來妳是個職業歌手呀。

B：噢，我可不敢說是個職業歌手，但在學校我確實受過一些訓練。我的音樂老師曾經是位職業歌手。

A：哦，名師出高徒啊！

B：這話你說得對！

深入分析

★no wonder 難怪

字面意思是「不用懷疑」，也就是「毫不奇怪」、「難怪」，表示先前猜測或評論是符合預期的，例如：

⊙No wonder he can win the game.

難怪他能贏得這場比賽。

MP3 132

實·用·會·話·6

A：What do you think of my new hat?

B：It's very nice. It goes beautifully with your dress.

A：Thank you. It's very nice of you to say so.

B：You're welcome.

A：My sister gave me this hat for my birthday.

B：She has excellent taste.

- - - - - - - - - - - - - - - -

A：你認為我的新帽子怎麼樣？

B：好看，配你的衣服很好看。

A：謝謝。你這樣說真是太好了。

B：不客氣。

A：這是我生日時，我姐姐送我的帽子。

B：她的品味很好！

★taste 品味

除了是「味道」的意思之外，也可以表示「審美力」、「鑑賞力」，例如：

⊙ She has excellent taste in dress.

她對衣著有極好的鑑賞力。

⊙ The lady dresses in perfect taste.

這位女士穿著的品味極佳。

永續圖書
線上購物網

www.foreverbooks.com.tw

◆ 加入會員即享活動及會員折扣。

◆ 每月均有優惠活動，期期不同。

◆ 新加入會員三天內訂購書籍不限本數金額，
即贈送精選書籍一本。（依網站標示為主）

專業圖書發行、書局經銷、圖書出版

永續圖書總代理：
五觀藝術出版社、培育文化、棋茵出版社、犬拓文化、讀
品文化、雅典文化、知音人文化、手藝家出版社、瓊申文
化、智學堂文化、語言鳥文化

活動期內，永續圖書將保留變更或終止該活動之權利及最終決定權。

職場英文王:會話能力進階手冊

20個最常見的商務主題
各個主題的架構如下:
1. 關於各主題的簡介:各章學習前的暖身準備,幫助讀者進入狀況。
2. 脈絡分明的常用表達方式:分門別類整理常用句型,加上言簡意賅的提示。
3. 切合主題的情境對話:幫助讀者於自然情境中學習,潛移默化將英語用法快速記牢。
4. 重點字彙庫:字彙是由情境對話中擷取出的重要常用單字,並且附有音標和字義。

貼心小叮嚀:貼心提醒各主題實務所該注意的事項,特別強調文化差異與溝通技巧。

商業實用英文 E-mail-業務篇 + 文字光碟

E-mail商用書信No.1的選擇!
分門別類規劃商業主題,
查詢方便,主題、例句馬上套用,
快速完成一封商務E-mail
E-mail for Business

旅遊英語萬用手冊

想出國自助旅遊嗎?
不論是 出境、入境、住宿,
或是 觀光、交通、解決三餐,
通通可以自己一手包辦的「旅遊萬用手冊」!

生活英語萬用手冊

英語學習不再是紙上談兵！
背誦單字的同時，也能學習生活中最常用的短語對話，讓英語學習更生活化、更有效率！

跟莎士比亞一學就會的 1000 單字

透過莎士比亞的戲劇，無痛學會 1000 個好用的單字、片語和短語！
英語世界傳世的文學作品，除了探討人生與人性，更蘊含人文學和語言之美，無疑是學習英語的優良教材，適合每一個對英語有興趣的學習者。

抓住文法句型，翻譯寫作就通了

本書之編寫旨在針對英文中常見之文法句型做一簡明及重點式的介紹，不管是在校的學生們，抑或是職場上的社會人士，熟讀本書不僅可對重要的文法句型快速入門，如能對每一個文法句型所附上的文法及翻譯練習題加以實際的演練，對於翻譯及寫作將有紮實的幫助，同時也有助於對英文文章大架構及文意瞭解之增進。

Good morning很生活的英語

雅致風靡　典藏文化

親愛的顧客您好，感謝您購買這本書。即日起，填寫讀者回函卡寄回至本公司，我們每月將抽出一百名回函讀者，寄出精美禮物並享有生日當月購書優惠！想知道更多更即時的消息，歡迎加入"永續圖書粉絲團"您也可以選擇傳真、掃描或用本公司準備的免郵回函寄回，謝謝。

傳真電話：（02）8647-3660　　　　電子信箱：yungjiuh@ms45.hinet.net

姓名：			性別：	□男　　□女
出生日期：　年　　月　　日			電話：	
學歷：			職業：	
E-mail：				
地址：□□□				
從何處購買此書：			購買金額：　　　　元	
購買本書動機：□封面 □書名□排版 □內容 □作者 □偶然衝動				
你對本書的意見： 內容：□滿意□尚可□待改進　編輯：□滿意□尚可□待改進 封面：□滿意□尚可□待改進　定價：□滿意□尚可□待改進				
其他建議：				